Cyndi

Jamila D. Smith

ISBN: 1492119954
ISBN 13: 9781492119951

Dedication:

This book is dedicated to my mom, Connie
Smith, for all her blood, sweat, and tears
And:
To my father, Howard B. Smith, who didn't see this
project come to fruition (Rest in Peace) I miss you!!!

Acknowledgements:

I want to send a **HUGE** thank you to my models and their parents, who participated with this project. Thank you so much:

Manea Allen, Shannon Billups, Terence Billups, and Selena Brooke King. Also, to the owner of the La-Z-Boy Service Center; on Cane Run Road in Louisville, Ky.

Chapter 1
1995

For as long as I can remember, I grew up as a foster child in Brooklyn, New York. I was told that my mother died while giving birth to me on a brutally cold winter night during a blizzard. Based on what the foster care professionals had told me, she died at the age of 18 in New Jersey. When she died, there weren't any other siblings because her family wasn't anywhere to be found. Plus my father disappeared before I was born. So there basically wasn't any chance of me having any contact with him either.

The only facts that I knew about my parents were that my mother was African-American and my father was Jamaican. So, I always assumed that explained my unique features my large, almond-shaped, brown eyes, narrow nose, high cheek bones, and natural-textured hair. My complexion was as rich as a Hershey candy bar and my lips were almost as full as the beautiful actress, Meagan Good. Many people often approached me and assumed that I was an African immigrant, because of my unique features and tall, slim build. However, I would often reply, "No, I'm a Jamaican American," because I truly believed that I was, despite the fact I barely knew my ancestral background.

From the time I was a new born, I was placed in foster care around the country. But now, at age eight, I lived in Brooklyn and hated this place with a passion. People were rude and often tried to hustle and con one another. I couldn't stand how girls could be so treacherous, or how the older boys used their doggish charm to get girls out of their pants. Despite these behaviors, I had many moments when I could mentally escape and dream of becoming a doctor, once I grew up. My biggest fantasy was to leave this hell hole and fly away without ever turning back. Lying in bed deep in thought about this chosen fantasy when I should have been dressing for school one day, I was suddenly interrupted by my best friend, Martina.

"Cyndi, hurry up, before Ms. Francis gets us! You know she's gonna be pissed off if she catches you in your pajamas!" she cried, bursting into the bedroom we shared with two other girls.

"Man, forget that ol' witch. I'll do whatever I wanna do!" I smarted off, rolling my eyes.

"She's gonna get you, so you better hurry your ass up!" Martina advised again.

"Alright! Damn!" I said impatiently.

I was about to get up and slip on a pair of jeans, but I was too late. Ms. Francis appeared in the doorway, before I could do anything. She was an amazing woman, in her late 50s and using a cane to steady her limp. Rumors were rampant that her husband used to beat her many years ago. But that limp never stopped her. Ms. Francis was still able to get around.

"What are you two doing in here?" she demanded with one hand on her hip, as the other clutched the cane. "Martina, didn't I tell you to wake the other kids around the facility for school? Go on and do what I told you to do!"

"Yes, ma'am," Martina replied in fear as she hurried out of the room.

Everyone was afraid of her, but I wasn't. Instead, I often challenged her.

"And you," she said turning to me. "You get your narrow tail up and get dressed. Do I make myself clear? We're not going through this again. Do you understand me?"

"Please! Your old self can't make me," I said defiantly with a smirk.

"Excuse me?" she asked, stepping toward me.

"Did I stutter? I said..." Unfortunately I was slapped on my bare thighs with her cane. I was still dressed in my sweat-shirt and underwear, wearing only one sock.

"Ow!" I cried, rubbing my legs where it stung.

"Get up!" she ordered.

"Nooo!" I refused.

"You get yourself up or..." she raised her cane in mid air until I ran.

"Nooo!" I yelled as I ran toward the hallway.

"Get back here!" she yelled, chasing me.

"You know you can't catch me for real," I snickered as my pace increased.

Kids who were preparing for school or having breakfast soon came out to see the commotion. I was enjoying it, but Ms. Francis wasn't. Her fury continued to rise. She experienced battles with us on a daily basis, but I was the worst. Many kids would try stunts with her, but eventually she was able to manage them once she caught them. On the contrary,

I was quick as a bullet. Martina had once told me that I should become a track star.

"Come back here and get dressed!" she yelled continuing to chase me as she wobbled on her cane.

Other kids soon began to chant, "Go Cyndi! Run!"

Martina stood in the hallway, smirking. She wanted to laugh out loud, but was afraid.

I ran down the stairs, through the double doors that lead to the kitchen, around the stove area, and down the second flight of stairs to the recreation room. She chased me through every room of the house, clutching my clothes, while I continued to run like a savage child in my sweatshirt and underwear. Suddenly, a whistle blew and everyone froze in silence, which caused me to stop in my tracks. It was Big Mike.

"Big Mike" got his nick- name because he was tall and broad like Mike Tyson. He was a 40-year- old, 6'4" man with a mahogany complexion. Big Mike always wore his hair slick back into a ponytail. He was half Puerto Rican and half African American. He was also known for beating girls like a runaway slave, if they refused to follow the rules of the facility. Or, he would send them to the dark isolation room where kids had limited access to food and socialization.

Ms. Francis' son, Big Mike gave me a hard glare as he said, "Cyndi, you have exactly three seconds to march yourself upstairs and put on some clothes. Move!"

I snatched my clothes from Ms. Francis and stomped toward the stairs, with laughter waiting to escape from within.

"You know you're too old to be running around like that in front of these boys. What the hell is wrong with you?" he yelled.

"I guess I don't know any better, huh?" I smarted off with a sneer as I ascended the staircase.

Other kids began to laugh hysterically until he ordered them to, "Shut up!"

Ms. Francis wobbled into her office to probably write a report on me, but I didn't care. The house eventually became quiet and kids went back to doing their morning rituals. Martina came into our room laughing.

"You're so bad Cyndi! I can't believe you did that! You know Big Mike was ready to beat your ass for real."

"I know it, but I don't care," I said, finally slipping on my jeans.

"You should. I thought it was over for you," Martina said.

"Nah, not really," I said, smiling devilishly. "I'm just gettin' started."

"What do you mean?"

"She still has to catch me after school today. And that's gonna be funny as hell," I said, beginning to tie my sneakers.

"Cyndi, you're bad!" Martina laughed.

After styling my hair into pigtails with my favorite pink ribbons, I grabbed my book bag as Martina made my bed. Each morning we were supposed to get up at 6:30 to exercise, clean our rooms, and eventually dress for school. But since our school didn't start until 9:30, I felt that it was pointless to get up so early. Instead, I woke up an hour and a half later, which led me to always being behind in my morning duties.

Martina and I always looked out for one another. She was the sister that I could never have. We ended up becoming friends one day when I took the punishment for her after she fought another resident. She and the other girl fought over money. In the end, the girl backed down with a bloody lip and a broken arm, whereas I had to go without food and water for two days. Big Mike had insisted that I should confess to how the fight started.

"I know there's more to what you're telling me," he accused. "What really happened?"

"I don't know!" I denied.

"Well, maybe this will jog your memory," he threatened. He suddenly shoved me down the stairs, which lead to bruising my elbow.

I howled in pain.

"You ready to talk now?" he asked, hatefully.

"No!"

"Whatever, I don't have time for this," he said, now jerking on my arm as he lifted me up. He started to drag me to a dark, padded room known as the chamber room.

He shoved me inside as my head rammed into the wall. "You can forget about going to that pizza party tonight!" he soon slammed the door and I was welcomed by darkness as I cried in pain and fear.

To this day, the other girl no longer bullies Martina nor steals from us. But I was extremely terrified of Big Mike. His presence would now bring back memories of being shoved down the wooden stairs and sleeping inside that cold, dark torture chamber. That was three months ago and Martina and I had been best friends ever since. She was Latino and appeared meek since she was so tiny. Kids always tried to initiate fights with her, assuming that she was timid. Yet Martina had a temper that could be really destructive, so much so that the staff had been ready to transfer her to another facility. Rather than seeing Martina be sent off to a place that would torture her worse, I decided to take the heat for her behavior that day.

On other occasions, Martina had taken the blame for my actions as well, so it was a give and take friendship. There was a time when Big Mike once stuck her hand in a pot of boiling water when neither of us admitted that I intentionally pulled the fire alarm. It was his idea of showing the girls the consequences of pulling a prank. Martina decided to succumb to having blisters on her hands for a month simply so I wouldn't experience another beating. Since our friendship was give and take, we would give and take each other's pain.

My best friend was petite with long, thick, jet black hair that hung past her shoulders. She had a bronze complexion and a strong Latino accent. I always believed that Martina should have been a supermodel; however, she often said that I was prettier. The only feature that I admired about myself was my hair, since I could style it in many different ways. There were times when I would wear micro braids, or kinky twists, or sometimes rock the twist out style. Many girls would torment me and demand to know if I wore a weave since it was so thick.

"You know your hair is fake, so don't even try to front," they would say. "I bet you have a bald head under all that hair. Maybe you have leukemia," another girl snickered.

"And maybe you'll have a split lip if you don't shut the fuck up!" I threatened.

Martina and I gave each other a hug and sung the song, *Ol' Mary Mack* as we finished up in our room that morning. Toward the end of the song, we hugged again, giggled, and grabbed our bags. Then we fled down the stairs to have our breakfast and run off to school.

Chapter 2

That Wednesday morning was off to a bad start for me right away. At recess, I was sent to the principal's office for fighting a boy, Taj Davidson, who I couldn't stand. He was in my third grade class and had a crush on me. But I was quick to let him know that his elementary puppy love feelings were not mutual. The minute he tried to kiss me on the playground, I slapped him across the face.

Ms. Hill, our teacher, didn't see him when he hit me back, but unfortunately saw me when I struck him in the gut and kicked him in his shin.

"Cyndi Taylor, you can march yourself to Mr. Miller's office. That type of behavior is unacceptable!" she ordered.

"Ooh! I hate this school!" I cried, stomping the pavement toward the building.

I was fuming not only because Taj made the moves on me, but because he never got caught and had the nerve to laugh in my face as he watched me report toward my possible expulsion.

"Shut up!" I snarled at him.

Mr. Miller knew me quite well. It seemed as though we had weekly visits since I constantly stayed in trouble.

"What happened this time, Cyndi?" he asked, ready to hear my long string of excuses as I was called into the office.

"I didn't do it Mr. Miller! It was Taj. He started it!" I stated becoming defensive. "I hate him!"

"Calm down and tell me what happened," Mr. Miller requested.

I slumped in the chair that sat directly in front of his desk and pouted, as I told my version of the story.

"I was playin' jump rope with Kendra and Stephanie and Taj and his friend, Corey, ran up to me and smacked me," I explained, remembering every detail. "Corey pulled my hair and Taj hit me. When I hit him back, he tried to kiss me, but I gave him my fist, and a good kick and then Corey laughed."

Mr. Miller continued to listen, wanting to chuckle at the situation.

"Then Ms. Hill caught me and told me to go to the office, but I didn't do nothin'. Taj started it!" I raged.

"It's possible that he did start it," Mr. Miller said. "He may have been bothering you on the playground and you can best believe that I will speak to him about this, too. But what I want you to understand, Cyndi, is that as a third grader, you need to be making better choices," Mr. Miller lectured. "You can't always solve your problems by fighting other class-mates. This past week you've been in quite a few fights with Taj. I want to see you start making better choices. Because one more incident, and you're outta here. Do I make myself clear?" he ordered.

"Yeah," I mumbled, not appreciating the lecture. Mr. Miller always carried himself with that *la-la land* mentality.

"Cyndi," he called before I walked out. "The next time Taj starts to bother you again, you let your teacher handle him so that you don't end up coming back to the office again. Can you do that?"

"Yeah, alright," I replied.

When school was out, Martina and I decided to take our good ol' time getting back to the home. She fretted over needing to get her report card signed, but I didn't buy in. "I'm really scared, Cyndi," she cried. "You know Big Mike gets mad if we get bad grades."

"Who cares? Come on, let's go to the park. I don't feel like seein' Big Mike anyway," I said, tugging her along.

School was out at 3:00, but we didn't return until 6:30.

"You know we're gonna get it, right?" Martina warned.

"So," I said, rolling my eyes.

"So where have the two of you been? Do you know what time it is?" Big Mike demanded the minute we walked in the door.

Martina tried to come up with a lie. "I left my jacket at school and had to go back and get it."

"Get to your room, Martina. I'll deal with you later," he ordered.

"But we didn't do nothin'. All we did was look for my jacket since it was lost," she defended while exchanging glances with me.

"I said to get to your room!" he yelled, shoving her. "And you, get upstairs," he said, facing me.

"Why?" I asked, suddenly becoming fearful.

"You ask way too many questions. And I'm sick of your smart- ass mouth. Get upstairs."

Reluctantly, I did what I was told. Martina, instead, went to the recreation room, which resulted in me being alone with Big Mike. Our other two roommates were studying outside.

"So, I hear that you've been fighting again. You just can't seem to follow the rules, can you?" he asked.

"He started it!" I yelled, referring to Taj.

"That's not the issue. Plus I hear that you've been kissing other boys."

"No I didn't! He tried to kiss me until I went to punch his ass out!" I yelled.

"That's enough. You act too grown and you have a big- ass mouth. You wanna see what happens to girls who talk too much?" He suddenly removed his belt and began to strike at me.

"Stop!" I cried.

"You try to run the streets like some wild child, so I'll have to treat you like one." Big Mike's strikes became fierce lashes. He swung the belt buckle at me, leaving welts on my arms and legs. I began to wail.

"You think you're better than the other girls around here? The hell you are. I know about your past," he said.

Big Mike continued to strike at me like I was his runaway slave. I ran into a corner and tried to block his blows, until Ms. Francis suddenly called him.

"Mike, I need your help on this one! I got two boys who went AWOL on us. You know what this means!" she called.

Big Mike soon gathered himself and began to head toward the doorway. Before he left, he grabbed my hair. "Consider yourself lucky. I was about to send you to the chamber room again." Big Mike's grip was so tight, that I was sure that my hairline would be ripped off at any moment.

"But, I'll deal with you later," he threatened as he walked out. "I'm on my way!" he yelled toward Ms. Francis.

I sat in the corner crying angry tears. If only I were three times his size. He would have been dead, I thought.

Chapter 3

The next day was better for me. Ms. Francis didn't have to chase me, and I didn't get into trouble with Big Mike. My teacher, Ms. Baker, also commented on my nice attire and positive behavior in the classroom, which helped with boosting my self-esteem.

"You look very pretty today, Cyndi," she complimented.

"Thanks."

"I want to see you make better choices today. Can you do that?" Ms. Baker encouraged.

I couldn't wait to see what she had in her treasure box that day. " If I do, can I get a candy?" I asked, eagerly.

"We'll see," she said, smiling.

I sat at my desk and suddenly became more motivated to complete my assignment.

That day I wore blue jean overalls with a white, short-sleeved shirt. My red, plaid shirt was tied around my waist to match my *Filas* sneakers. I had my hair pulled into a ponytail with slick bangs in the front, trying to resemble my favorite artist, Aaliyah. Martina had styled my hair earlier that morning when she woke up. Her dream was to become a beautician one day.

"I'm sorry I smacked you yesterday," Taj said to me during recess.

"You better be, 'cause I was ready to stomp your ass," I said, becoming angry again.

"Tag, you're it!" he announced, smacking me on the arm and running.

"Hey!" I yelled, chasing after him.

From that day on, I grew to like him, but refused to show it. Each time he stared at me in class, I rolled my eyes or stuck out my tongue. He would laugh and return his focus to his class work. Taj now seemed perfect to me since we had things in common. We both were in third grade and were the same age and had the same homeroom teacher.

Taj was tall and skinny with a peanut butter complexion and hazel eyes. He had a short hair-cut with a blonde streak on the side. His Brooklyn accent was thick and he had the cutest smile, along with his class-clown demeanor.

"OK, boys and girls, I need for all of you to write a paragraph on what you want to be when you grow up," Ms. Baker announced.

This assignment wasn't difficult for me since I constantly day-dreamed about my future. It was my only coping mechanism to escape from my nightmare life in the shelter. I was the first one to finish my paper. Once I completed the assignment, I sat at my desk with my hands folded. When Ms. Baker wasn't looking, I threw a balled up piece of paper at Taj. Rather than retaliating, Taj ignored me and continued to write his paper.

"OK, Cyndi, since you seem to be quite feisty, you can be the very first one to present your paper," Ms. Baker said.

"OK," I agreed.

Taj made a funny face and I laughed. I stood up in front of the class and read, "When I grow up I want to be a doctor and live in a big house and marry Marcus Houston from Immature. I want to have a dog named Foxy and have a nice car. The reason I want to be a doctor is because I want to help people when they get sick, and then I want to have my dog bite crazy people like Taj," I emphasized, staring at him.

"Thank you for sharing your paper, Cyndi. Good job," she praised.

Then it was Taj's turn. He read his response and finished with, "I wanna be a comedian like Martin Lawrence when I grow up," Taj read, smiling. "Because, I like to make people laugh. And then I want to live in California and have two big dogs to bite the robbers who wanna rob my house."

"Very good Taj. Eric, you're next," Ms. Baker said to another student.

"Oh please, you know that you'll never be like Martin 'cause your jokes ain't even funny," I joked.

Deep down inside, I truly loved his paper, but refused to let him know.

"Yes I will. I'm gonna make big Benjamins, too!" Taj said, becoming defensive.

"Of course you'll become an important person. All of you will succeed, because I know that each of you has a lot of potential," Ms. Baker said.

When school was out, I met Martina at the playground. We normally met there after school since we hardly saw each other during school hours. Both of us had different teachers and separate recess schedules.

"What's wrong?" I asked. I sensed that she was upset before she could open her mouth.

"I'm in trouble again. Big Mike saw my report card and made me sit in the chamber room yesterday and I couldn't eat. And then he made me stay on my knees," she said sadly. "He said if I got another bad grade I would get a whoopin' and have to stay on my knees again!"

"Oh no!" I cried, realizing what she was referring to.

Martina soon revealed her bloody knees. The other day, Big Mike caught her stealing food from the kitchen after dinner time. When she was caught red-handed, he made her kneel on grains of dry cereal on the kitchen tile until she promised that she would never steal again.

"I got an F on my spellin' test today 'cause Ms. Shields caught me cheatin'. She made me take it home to get it signed. But I don't wanna take it home. I don't wanna get in trouble again, Cyndi! I'm scared!" she cried.

"It's OK, you won't get in trouble. Gimme me your paper."

"Why?" she asked.

"Just do it."

Cautiously, she handed it to me and I snatched it from her. I ripped the paper in several tiny pieces and tossed it in the garbage can. "This is to Big Mike," I said, spitting on the remains.

"Here's to Big Mike," she repeated.

Once we tore up her document, I saw that she instantly felt relieved. She gave me a hug and we began to sing our song, *Ol' Mary Mack*. Martina and I giggled and headed off to play in the park. We didn't care about getting in trouble. Facing a consequence at home was always a possibility regardless of if we indulged in trouble or not. As we headed toward a set of swings, a group of other kids appeared with a stereo and played songs by Notorious B.I.G. Eventually the group grew and some chose to dance to the sounds of *Big Poppa.*

Martina had mentioned that she was sent to the chamber room the day before. She never talked much when she was upset instead, she often remained withdrawn. But whenever we sat together, she would tell me her deepest, darkest secrets from her past. She would talk about of how she witnessed her entire family get shot by drug dealers. Martina told me that she hid under her bed and played possum, which kept her from being killed. As we sat in the park, I imagined seeing Big Mike get gunned down by one of the older kids dancing there.

Chapter 4

1999

Now that I was 12, I noticed the changes that were occurring all around me more. Martina and I were still close, but she was different. It was as if she and I had matured at separate paces. Instead of coming across as a timid push over, she was now more aggressive. Martina was still short, but she liked wearing a lot of make-up and dressing in urban gear and baggy clothes. Her innocent demeanor had now been replaced with promiscuity. Her body had also physically developed much quicker than mine, and she was extremely boy crazy. I on the other hand, felt as if Mother Nature took her time with me.

I felt so under developed and boyish. The only physical attribute that I admired about myself was my hair, since I could still wear it in versatile styles. It had grown down to my shoulders, and I was much taller. Martina had insisted that I was the best looking girl in our math class, but I couldn't see it, since I still wore a training bra. Ms. Francis continued wobbling about the facility and Big Mike was still beating the residents, but he no longer bothered me or Martina.

"Guess what, girl? I've been checkin' your boy out. You know he's got it goin' on with his fine ass!" Martina laughed, smacking her gum, as she sat on my bed.

Although she took extra time with primping herself into a diva with her make-up, fancy hair-do, and nails, Martina was always ready for school before I was. Therefore, she never minded waiting on me in the mornings.

"Who?" I asked.

"Girl, let me do that," she offered, starting to braid my hair. "I'm talkin' about Hakim in Mr. Keller's class. I heard that boy's got mad paper!"

"He's alright," I said, nonchalantly.

"I think his boy likes you," she sang.

"Who?" I asked, spinning around to face her.

"Taj Davidson! I always see him starin' at your ass when you walk in the hallway."

"Whatever," I laughed.

"I'm serious, girl! You better hurry and get up on that before somebody else does," Martina said, gyrating humorously. 'Cause you know that's your man."

"Please," I said, sarcastically.

"You girls need to stop flappin' your jaws about these boys and start gettin' ready for school!" Ms. Francis yelled from the stairway.

"She needs to start flappin' about gettin' a new leg," I muttered.

"Alright, Ms. Francis!" Martina laughed.

"I'm not laughin'. You girls think that life is a joke. But in reality, these boys ain't about nothin' except for gettin' girls pregnant," Ms. Francis lectured.

"Whatever. I can handle my own," Martina smarted.

"I ain't that stupid," I said defensively.

I truly felt that I would never have the "ideal boyfriend" or get asked to the school dance. Martina was the one who collected all the phone numbers of boys she met, and had boys spending money on her.

"That's what I said before I had my son," she said before walking away.

"Anyway, girl, Hakim is the shit! It's on tonight!" Martina continued, referring to their so-called date.

Their fellatio encounters always occurred in the boys' locker room after school.

"I guess he's alright," I agreed.

Martina and I ended up going to school for half the day, but ditched the afternoon. Instead we went to our favorite spot to hang out in the back of an abandoned grocery store.

"Man, I can't wait until tonight. It's been forever since I had some," Martina said, puffing on our blunt.

She was already high and we had only started smoking 15 minutes ago.

"Where will you go?" I asked, after accepting my turn.

"Hell if I know. Maybe me and Hakim could go to a library. I've never done it there before," she laughed.

"Hakim must be a serious freak," I said, snickering. I was already getting contact.

"If you only knew!" Martina laughed hysterically.

After finishing our blunt, we tried singing our childhood song again, *Ol' Mary Mack,* but forgot the words since we were high.

"Man, fuck this shit. I can make up my own rap!" I said, beginning to freestyle as she created a beat.

Both of us broke out into huge laughter and passed out. We slept for nearly two hours. Once we woke up, we decided to indulge in more mischief.

"Let's go to the park," I suggested.

"Cool. But I'm hungry as hell, though. We need to hustle for some grub for real," Martina said.

"Most def," I agreed.

Although we were at a crossroads between childhood to adolescence, we still enjoyed hanging out at our favorite playground on the swings. Many fun activities occurred there such as, parties, dance contests, basketball games and freestyle tournaments. Martina and I could have cared less about getting in trouble at home.

She was too involved in her mission of finding a potential one-nightstand for the day as I searched for dudes to give us more green to smoke. After tricking two high school dudes into giving us cash, we bought ourselves a snack.

"Hey, I wanna play basketball," Martina announced once she finished her hot dog.

"*You* wanna play basketball?" I asked, humorously.

Martina was never into sports. She didn't like to sweat off her make-up. But, today my friend was full of unexpected surprises.

"Hell yeah!" she said, excitedly.

"You know you don't like goin' to basketball games at school, so I know you really lost your mind if you say you wanna play," I said, cautiously.

What was she really up to?

"Whatever, I like playin' ball and so do you," she said, tugging my arm.

Before I could resist, I soon realized that we were joining Taj and Hakim on the court. They had just arrived shortly after we did.

"Are you ready to lose?" Hakim asked.

"Naw, that's what I should be askin' you!" I said, stepping up into Taj's face.

"It's on," Hakim challenged.

Toward the end of the game, it came to a tie.

"Now, that's your lesson for havin' too much pride. You know we can slam dunk your asses for real," I said laughing.

"Whatever, we ended up lettin' you guys win," Taj said, smirking.

"Why don't you guys come back tomorrow so we can really show you what we're about," Hakim challenged.

"Bet, it's on," I said, standing in Taj's face again. 'Cause I'm gonna be shovin' my foot up your ass anyway, you just wait."

The next day Martina and I decided to attend the entire day at school, since we'd nearly missed six days in a row. During our math lecture, I noticed Taj staring at me. Whenever I stared back, he immediately turned away and returned to his notes. This went on everyday for nearly a week and I would always become annoyed. Taj was beginning to drive me crazy and it was confusing. Last year we couldn't stand each other and now, all of a sudden, he would give long stares, which really irked me.

I finally decided to handle this. This situation had gone on long enough. When class ended, I marched directly to him and demanded to know why he had a staring problem.

"Aye, I wanna know what's your problem? What's up?" I asked defensively, with my hands posed on my hips. "You got a starin' problem or somethin'?"

"Nah, not really." Taj shrugged. "I just like lookin' at you, that's all. You got a problem with that?" he asked, standing in my face.

For a minute I wasn't sure what to say. All I could do was stand in front of him with my guard up. I stared into his hazel eyes.

"Oh," I said, suddenly feeling embarrassed. "I like lookin' at you, too."

"I like lookin' at your hair," he said.

"And I like lookin' at your funny faces that you always make," I said.

"So?" Taj asked.

"So, let's do this," I insisted.

"Well, give me your number then," he said, continuing to stand in my face.

"No, you give me yours," I ordered.

Before I realized it, Taj had written his phone number down on a piece of notebook paper and slipped it into my hand, as he quickly kissed me. It wasn't our third-grade, playground kiss this time. Instead, we had a more puppy-love passion, that made our brief moment of chemistry appear longer.

My body experienced a ton of emotions that I had never experienced before. My breath was caught up in my throat, my legs became wobbly, and my stomach did flip flops. I could feel my heart pounding heavily and I suddenly had to use the restroom due to excitement. I had experienced my first kiss. I would never forget this feeling. How I had wished that I could encounter it one more time. Instead, it was my first and last memory of Taj.

Chapter 5

Taj was killed that very same day. He hadn't even made it home to receive my phone call. On his way to make a drug run with Hakim they had, experienced a bad exchange. A group of older kids had ganged up Taj and robbed him. They beat him severely and shot him multiple times as they took his money, jewelry, and drug paraphernalia. Taj was only 12 years old and in the seventh grade.

The minute I received the news from Martina, I sobbed like a newborn baby. I was just about to sneak into Ms. Francis' office to grab the cordless and hide in the furnace room downstairs in the basement to make the call to Taj. Girls always communicated with their boyfriends there, because that was the very last place Big Mike or Ms. Francis would search to find us. Plus, having a boyfriend was never permitted, unless we wanted another reason for a beating.

Martina burst into our room with a tear-streaked face. Her eyes were blood-shot red and her mascara was smeared.

"Cyndi, did you hear what happened?" she asked.

"About what?"

"About Taj. He was." I cut her off.

"Yeah, I know. You don't have to tell me. He likes me. I finally got him to say it. So now I'm gonna go call him, so that I can hear his funny jokes."

"No, you can't," she said, trying to grasp my hand.

"What you mean, I can't?" Girl, you better move outta my way!" I ordered.

"You can't call him, Cyndi!" she cried.

"The hell I can't! Why not?" I asked, impatiently. She was beginning to kill my excitement.

"Because he's, he's," Martina stammered.

"Come on, what?" I asked, huffing.

She stood in front of me with tearful eyes.

"What?" I yelled, now becoming annoyed.

"Dead! Taj is dead. He was shot on Queens Boulevard!" she cried.

"No," I denied, shaking my head. "Stop playin'. You play too much. I just saw him at school, so I know you're full of shit!"

"You think I'm makin' this shit up?" she cried.

To reassure proof, another girl, who attended school with us, came into our room crying. She didn't have to reassure me. I read it from her face.

"Nooo!" I cried.

Martina tried to hug me, but I pushed her away and ran out. I ran past other kids out in the hallway, pushing them, and ran down the stairs toward the front door. I wasn't sure where I was going, but I allowed my feet to lead me to wherever they would take me, as they pounded on the pavement.

My vision was blurred with tears that burned under my eyelids, and streamed down my cheeks. My stomach ached, I heard people calling my name, but I didn't care. I blocked them out and continued running. I hadn't realized that I had run so far, but soon I discovered that I was heading to another section of town.

Mobs of people and dozens of police cars were crowded around a body lying at a basketball court at the park. It was Taj, lying in a pool of blood with bullet holes in his young body and scuff marks on his face that once was gorgeous. I had made it there before the police covered him up with a sheet.

I continued to run, still shoving people who were in my way, as I cried. His eyes were still open with evidence of the horrid death. I ran to his limp body and grabbed his hand, hoping that I could get one last word, or a forced smile that I would miss forever. I wanted to shout, "Wake up! I still have to call you tonight!"

But instead, all I could do was call out his name. "Taj! Taj!"

I felt someone seize me by my shoulders and drag me away. At that moment the officers covered his body.

"NOOO!"I yelled. "Leave me alone!"

"It's over, honey. He's gone," the officer said, sadly.

"No he's not!"I cried.

Just then, I saw blackness before me and passed out. The next thing I remember is waking up in a cold, quiet hospital room. I heard low voices whispering outside the room. I assumed someone was talking about me.

Where was I? How did I get here? Just when I was about to get up, my body collapsed back down onto the pillow.

"I have to get outta here," I said.

Suddenly, I saw Taj's figure in the doorway. He stood there with a blank expression. "Taj," I said, reaching out toward him.

In the next moment he was gone and I began to cry. That's when a set of lights snapped on and a nurse came running in.

"Oh, you must have woken up. It's alright, honey," she said, hugging me.

I clung to her and cried like a baby again. Once I calmed down she gave me a Kleenex. My chest still ached, my eyes were puffy and sore, and my stomach felt tight. Plus, my throat was dry. It hurt to talk. I assumed all these symptoms were from long crying spells.

"Here, take this sweetheart. It'll make you feel better," she said, handing me a cup of water.

I took a huge gulp and tried to relax.

"Where am I? Where are my clothes?" I asked, suddenly realizing that I was wearing a hospital gown. "Ms. Francis is gonna be pissed that I ran off."

"Slow down, honey," the nurse said, soothingly. "You suffered from a black-out two hours ago, due to grief and stress. You really need to take it easy."

"Where are my clothes?" I asked.

For some reason, I was terrified of getting into trouble when I got home. I wanted to start the day over. Unfortunately it was too late.

"Your social worker has them," the nurse replied.

"My social worker? What the hell is goin' on?" I asked, confused.

"There's someone who needs to see you," she said.

Before I could reply my nurse who was so pleasant and supportive left me alone. A young, Italian lady who appeared to be in her early 30s appeared. She had long, thick, black hair that was pulled back into a ponytail and she carried my clothes in a clear, plastic bag.

"What's goin' on?" I demanded.

"Hey, I'm Gina. I'm gonna be your caseworker today," she informed. "Some new arrangements have been made for ya," she calmly stated.

"What kinda arrangements?" I asked.

"Before we get into that, I need to know what goes on in that shelter where you stay. And don't worry, you're safe now," she said.

I'd heard that line so many times, yet I would end up going to a place that was worse or crazier.

"I don't know what you're talkin' about," I denied, not trusting her.

"Cyndi, I have to know. There's been several cases of child endangerment and physical abuse among a ring of girls. I need to hear your side."

"I can't tell you," I said, tears forming.

"Has anyone ever hurt you?" she asked.

I sat in silence, still not sure whether to tell my life story or to remain silent. For all I knew, she could have sent me to another spot with a staff just as mean as Big Mike.

"Cyndi, it's OK," she reassured me when I refused to answer.

"Sometimes," I said through a sniffle.

"Who?" she asked.

I told her every horrid detail of what occurred from the time I was seven until my adolescent years. I had been slapped, shoved, burned, and restrained for several hours. I also was starved if I misbehaved or became belligerent. Then I blurted out about several occasions of witnessing other girls becoming physically injured by Big Mike. Just like the time when Martina was shoved into a coffee table when she was caught kissing a boy in the closet.

My social worker jotted everything I told her inside her notepad and then asked me to get dressed. "As soon as you finish, please meet me in the hallway. I'll explain everything once we're outside."

All I had on earlier was a pair of baggy jeans, a T-shirt, *Timberlands* and a denim jacket, so it didn't take me that long to get ready. Once I was dressed, I stepped outside of the room to join her.

"You did a very brave thing, Cyndi. You're safe now," she said as we walked out.

"I have to get back. Ms. Francis will give me hell, so we should hurry," I said, as we stepped into the county car.

"That's all over for you now," she informed, starting the car.

"What do you mean?"

"Based on what you told me, I have to remove you from your home and report what happened. My job is to make sure that you're placed in a safer environment," she explained.

"So what are you sayin'?" I asked, not ready to hear what was coming.

"There's a new family in the state of Rhode Island who wants to adopt you. We've met in person and spoke on the phone the other day. They seem really nice and they're ready to make the arrangements today," she said smiling.

I knew that she was trying her best to make things optimistic. But it wasn't happening. My environment where I had lived for the past four years was stable. It was the only home in which I had established respect and peer acceptance. Although it had its moments of chaos and occasional violence, I was now accustomed to it. Moving away would only lead to starting over, which was never a pleasant experience. I was tired of moving.

"I'm not," I said, defensively.

"Well, you should be, Cyndi. They're your family and they're ready to take you in," Gina was now becoming blunt for some reason.

"I don't have a *real* family," I snarled.

"You do," she insisted.

"How do you know?" I asked, not believing her.

"You have a sister."

"I have a sister! No way!" I shrieked. "OK, if I supposedly have a sister, then why did these people decide to adopt me after 12 years? Can you tell me that?"

"I wish I could get into that, but I can't. Based on what they told me, it's a complicated story. So, I'll leave it up to them to explain it to ya," she answered.

I had the impression that she was now becoming uncomfortable.

"Uh hmm," I said, rolling my eyes.

We rode in silence for the rest of the ride until we pulled up in front of the shelter, where I would now leave without a trace. Some of my best friends were here and I couldn't bear to leave them. We always looked out for one another. I sat in a daze until Gina spoke up again.

"Cyndi, I need for you to go inside and gather your things. I'll be waiting in the office filling out some papers," she instructed.

This was crazy! It was all happening so fast. Surely I wasn't really leaving. Maybe I was dreaming. In a moment I would wake up and find myself in class day-dreaming and Taj would tell a funny joke. Or, Martina and I would be skipping school, hanging out at the playground again.

But instead, I wasn't dreaming. I was about to face my nightmare and go live with a group of strangers ,who never cared that I was alive for the past 12 years. My mind was in a trance, as I walked inside and went upstairs to my room.

"Cyndi, we have your belongings downstairs," Big Mike announced from the doorway.

This was all happening too fast. I wanted it to stop.

"Nooo!" I cried, running out of the room.

He tried to grab me, but I was too quick.

"Get back here!" he ordered.

I ignored him and continued to run until I found Martina in the recreation room.

"So it's true. You're really leavin', huh?" she sadly asked.

"Yeah," I answered in tears.

"Where you goin'?" she asked.

"Somewhere in Rhode Island. Can you believe that I actually have a real family?" I cried.

"That's good. You've always wanted to leave here anyway. Now this is your chance."

"I don't wanna leave you here," I cried.

"Don't worry about me. I'll be alright," she said, suddenly becoming tough. "Here, take this and always keep it. 'Cause if you lose it, I'll whoop your ass," she smiled through tears.

She ended up giving me her address on a small piece of bubble gum paper. A brand new joint was wrapped inside.

"I was about to use it before you came in," Martina explained.

"Here, you take this," I said, offering my pink ribbon. I've always kept it on me since I've had it ever since I was an infant.

"No," she resisted. "You know your ma probably wanted you to keep that."

"My mom is dead, so it doesn't matter. Besides, you're my sister. So, you keep it until we see each other again. Don't lose it, or it's your ass," I insisted.

"I promise," she replied.

Once again we sung our childhood song, *Ol' Mary Mack*, as a final farewell and hugged. Martina began to cry, but didn't want to show her tears.

"Go," she ordered, shoving me away.

I ran from her and tried to take off. Only this time, Gina who had been waiting for me, caught me. She tried to lead me to the car as Big Mike placed my suitcases inside the trunk.

"Get off me! Get off!" I cried, becoming violent.

Big Mike tried to intervene. "Cyndi, shut up and do what you were told!"

"That's enough. You've done more than enough already," Gina fired at him. As I continued to resist, she tried to console me.

"Cyndi, if you can't calm down and cooperate, I'll have to place you at a program where they help kids with controlling their anger. Is that what you want?" she asked.

I didn't answer, but soon became calm, trying to process what she was telling me.

"I know that you've lived at tons of shelters where you've had nothing but pain. But, I don't want to see you go through another bad experience again. Can you get it together?" she asked.

"Yeah," I scowled.

"OK, let's not blow your chances of getting into a better home. Your people are waiting on you."

"Alright," I answered.

"OK, let's get going," she said.

Reluctantly, I did what I was told. As I took my last glance, I turned and saw Martina standing in the window with tears flowing down her cheeks. I realized at that moment that I had to be strong. We stared at each other and silently mouthed our song. I watched her sing along, until I turned away and began to bawl hysterically.

Chapter 6

*O*ur route to Providence, Rhode Island was a little over three and a half hours from Brooklyn. Eventually I fell asleep on the way there, trying to block out everything that happened earlier. As soon as the car came to a halt, I woke up and stared at a three-story, black and white house with a double car garage and curved drive way.

There was a tennis court on the side and a swimming pool in the rear. I could hear chatter from the back, as water splashed loudly. Tall maple trees shaded the entire front lawn. We had arrived as the sun began to set.

"Who the hell lives here?" I asked, glancing around.

I expected to be entering a celebrity's crib with a soap opera home like this. It was so quiet and peaceful, with nature running so wild and free and birds chirping happily.

"You'll be living here now," Gina smiled.

I continued to look around, trying to adjust. This would be my new home. Hopefully it would welcome me in return. A few seconds after she rang the doorbell, a middle-aged man with short, blonde hair and friendly blue eyes answered the door. He had it brushed back neatly, with every strand in place.

The man wore a red, silk robe that was tied at the side with black, silk pajama pants and matching slippers. A newspaper was clutched in his right hand. His wife and daughter stood on the red carpet stairs behind him. His wife reminded me of an actress. I had the impression that she wanted to resemble Heather Locklear.

A white towel was wrapped around her hair, and she stood in a white terry cloth robe. Her face was made up to the max, with every product from *Revlon* and her bare toes sported polished, cherry red tips. I wasn't sure if she was dressed for bed or a beach party. Perhaps she had to live in vanity 24/7. His daughter wore a magenta two-piece bathing suit, showing her perfect, smooth tan.

All I could do was stare and size her up, as the girl returned the same reaction. Here was my sister, who I perceived had a different life and personality from me. We continued to stare at each other in amazement. She had her father's eye color, but her cheek bones and other facial features were similar to mine.

We both were the same exact height with the same length of hair, but different textures. For once, I finally got to meet a European reflection of myself. Her hair was straighter with a deep brownish tint. She had the complexion of J-Lo. I noticed how her skin glowed under the light.

"Well, it's good that you finally made it," the man said, smiling as he let us in.

"Hello Mr. Kramer," Gina greeted.

"Hello. You'll have to excuse the way we're dressed," he informed. "I was just about to catch up on sports and listen to music in the den, while Brittney and Sylvia were entertaining guests at our pool party."

"I totally understand," Gina accepted.

"Would you like anything? Punch? Tea? Or anything to eat?" he offered.

"No thank you."

"Are you sure? You're welcome to join us," he insisted.

"No really, I'm OK, but thanks," she said.

"David! For goodness sake," his wife said abruptly. "She said no. So, shall we get down to business?"

"Sure," Gina agreed.

"OK, Brittney, why don't you show Cyndi around and make her feel at home," her father suggested, giving her a look. "You remember we talked about that earlier."

"Yes, daddy," she said sarcastically.

From that moment, I realized that she was accustomed to being pampered. Yet having me around would suddenly change things for her.

"Are you my father?" I asked.

"Yes, I am," he answered.

"Wait a minute, my father is Jamaican. You didn't tell me he was white!" I fired, staring at Gina for answers.

"Cyndi, not now," she said softly.

"Dad!" Brittney wailed.

Oh my God, what the heck was her problem? I thought.

"You two girls get acquainted, while we handle things," he said. "Sylvia," he continued, signaling for her to follow him into the other room.

Sylvia wore a look of horror, as though she had been slapped. Brittney ended up showing me her room which looked like it came out of a bedroom design magazine. She had posters up of her favorite pop artists, such as N'Sync, Back Street Boys, Britney Spears, Aaron Carter and Christina

Aguilera. Brittney also had a huge wardrobe of clothes and accessories from several famous fashion designers. Afterward, she showed me her parents' room which had a king-sized canopy bed draped in fuchsia fabric. Toward the end of our tour, she led me to her studio where I assumed, she danced. Finally, we reached my bedroom.

"I hope you like it. My mom had it stripped and redecorated a dozen times this week," Brittney said.

"I love it," I said, amazed.

"Good."

I had my own laptop, a CD player, white carpet that was soothing to my feet, and a walk-in closet that was big enough to be another bedroom.

I had a full-length mirror door on my closet and a full-sized bed that had a white comforter with multi- colored, embroidered designs.

"Well, I'm glad to see that you've gotten her use to everything. Would you like anything to eat, honey?" Sylvia asked from the doorway.

"No thank you," I said.

"Well, you must be tired. We'll leave you alone and let you rest, although, we don't have any clothes for you to change into," Sylvia commented. "Brittney can lend you a pair of her pajamas. Go on, honey," she urged her daughter.

"But do I have to?" Brittney whined.

"Yes," Sylvia emphasized. "Now hurry."

My first night here and already my sister didn't want to share with me. I could only imagine how the rest of my time would be like with her.

"That's OK, I'll just sleep in my T-shirt," I stated.

I was too tired to remove anything. All I wanted to do was fall in bed, even if my shoes were still on or not.

"OK, that's fine for now. But tomorrow will be a big day for you. You need a new wardrobe," Sylvia said.

"I don't need any new clothes," I stated, now feeling uncomfortable. She stared at my outfit as if I was wearing filthy rags.

"Oh, you actually have a long way to go with improving your appearance," she said, scanning me.

"I've dressed this way all my life and never had any problems," I said, impatiently.

"Well, that's about to be changed now, just like your last name. From now on, you'll be known as Cyndi Kramer instead of Cyndi Taylor. Good night," she added as she closed the door.

I wanted to run after her and fire multiple questions. If David is my father, why isn't he Jamaican? Or if David isn't my father, then who is? Why wasn't Brittney raised in any foster homes, whereas I was?

I was so confused, but also exhausted. Before I knew it, I collapsed onto the bed and fell asleep. Brittney had followed her mother to join their guests at the party.

I woke up the next morning to the chaos of Brittney complaining.

"I can t find my suede boots! Mom, have you seen them?" she yelled from the hallway.

"No sweetie, I'm sorry," Sylvia apologized.

"This sucks! I have to wear them so that me and my best friend, Kailey, can dress alike! Now what am I supposed to do?" she cried.

I suddenly rose and opened my door.

"What are you looking at?" she demanded.

"I wish the hell I knew. But right now I wish you'd shut the hell up. I'm tryin' to sleep," I snapped.

"Well close your door then!"

"No bitch, close your mouth!" I fired.

"Dad!" she called.

"Oh please, miss princess wants to tell on me, ooh I'm scared," I said, sarcastically.

The day had just started and I was already irritated, now that we were at each others' throats.

"Well, I'm glad to see that everyone has awakened. How did you sleep?" our father asked, appearing.

"I was sleepin' good until she started throwin' a hissy fit!" I spat, glaring at Brittney.

"Whatever! I told you to close your door. So get over it!"

"Bitch, why don't you get over it. You're the one who was cryin' over some dumb-ass boots!" I yelled.

"Can you believe her? Daddy, do something!" Brittney shrieked.

"OK girls, let's try to get along," he said, humorously. "Our first day together and already our girls are having their first fight," he laughed.

"It's not funny!" Brittney and I shouted in unison.

Chapter 7

After breakfast, Sylvia and I went shopping for new clothes. We shopped around for different shoes, bras from several designers, and other female necessities. She even bought me make-up and jewelry. Towards the afternoon, she scheduled a physical exam for me at a walk-in clinic.

"Are you having sex?" Sylvia asked while completing the medical forms.

I soon became offended, feeling as though she were trying to make accusations rather than being helpful. For many years, I was always accused of being promiscuous when I never had any physical contact with a boy until the other day when I kissed Taj.

"No!" I snapped.

"Ok, I just had to know. Mothers have to know these things," she explained.

"Whatever," I mumbled. I was used to looking after myself. Accepting constant supervision was going to be a bitter pill to swallow.

Once we left the clinic, Sylvia and I went to get a facial and manicure. I soon got a glimpse of how she and Brittney spent their days together.

"Brittney and I do this every Saturday," Sylvia said as we sat in the nail salon.

"And why couldn't Brittney come with us today?" I asked, but glad that she hadn't.

"She had swim lessons today, which is another thing we need to talk about. David and I want to have you participate in extracurricular activities," Sylvia said. "Your sister also takes piano and modeling classes. Hopefully you'll find something that interests you so that you can stay involved and out of trouble."

"I don't get into trouble," I stated.

"Well, according to your social worker yesterday, she gave us an earful on things you've indulged in," Sylvia reported. "We can start by talking about the number of times you've tried to run away, gotten into fights, and not to mention the multiple accounts of marijuana use. Need I go on?"

"Whatever. I stopped doin' all that shit a long time ago," I denied.

"Maybe you did. But to avoid any regression of behavior, we're going to make some changes," she said, smiling.

All these changes. I wasn't liking this at all. Why did I suddenly have to have parental supervision now? I was already half grown up! All I needed was another six years until I turned 18.

After getting our facials and manicures, she took me to an elaborate restaurant called *The Swan*. The atmosphere was peaceful and classy, with an orchestra that played melodies from *Chopin*.

Once we finished our salads and spaghetti platters, Sylvia and I went shopping for school supplies. She and David had already arranged the paperwork for me to start at my new school that following Monday.

"Oh, we forgot your hair appointment," she groaned, as if she lost a million dollars.

"I don't care," I replied, nonchalantly.

"But you should care. A lady always has to make a good impression. Boy, you have a long way to go!"

At first I didn't mind getting my hair styled, until her beautician used a treatment that didn't agree with my hair. Rather than changing my hair to a straighter texture like Brittney's, it did the reverse. My hair was as frizzy and matted as a poodle, making it difficult to even run a comb through it. I was ready to raise hell. I was traumatized.

"I don't care what you say, I'm not goin' out lookin' like this! I hate it!"

Sylvia wasn't sure what to say. "It's not as bad as you think. You just need to adjust to your new appearance," she said in denial. Sylvia knew my hair was a disaster. She was at a loss for words.

"Would you like for me to try using a hair thinning solution?" her beautician asked, nervously.

"No!" I fired in tears.

"Come on Cyndi, it's not as bad as it seems. Let's give it a try and see what happens," Sylvia pleaded.

"I can't do this," I said, crying.

"Sure you can," her beautician said, trying to convince me.

Eventually, I relented and allowed her hair stylist to continue experimenting on my hair. Unfortunately her chemicals weren't a perfect match. My hair that once was healthy, thick, and shiny became brittle and dry. She eventually had to cut it, since my follicles were now weak. I hated my new appearance. My new hairstyle was now similar to a man's haircut, which made me look like a boy, I felt. I stared at my reflection and wanted to cry.

"Really Cyndi, you're over reacting," Sylvia said. "We only wanted to style your hair so that we could make you look more..."

"White?" I asked.

"Come on, you're reading more into it than you realize. We just wanted to have you look more presentable," she explained, realizing that I was becoming more upset.

"Whatever, you just wanted to change my appearance so that I could look more 'presentable' in front of your friends. But instead, your hair- dresser now has me lookin' like a boy since she didn't know what she was doin'!" I yelled. "Thanks to her, she fucked up my hair more!"

"This has never happened to Brittney's hair," Sylvia excused.

"I don't give a fuck! I'm not Brittney!"

"Get used to it, you're going to wear your hair this way whether you like it or not," she said coldly.

"The hell I am. My hair is fucked up now!" I raged.

I jumped out of the seat and ran out. I knew that I was blowing my chances of staying with them, but I didn't care. Why did I have to change myself to accommodate them?

What was so wrong that they had to go the extra mile to strip my hair and cause me to look like a boy?

She ended up paying her beautician for the screwed up perm and texturizer and walked out. Sylvia was furious, but I didn't care. She didn't bother to acknowledge my feelings about my traumatic appearance. Sylvia and I went straight to our rooms without speaking to each other once we arrived home.

"Well, how did we enjoy our rendezvous this afternoon?" David asked as we walked in.

"It sucked!" I yelled, stomping up the stairs.

"I'd rather not talk about it, Dave," Sylvia said, heading toward her room.

A little while later, I was called to dinner, but refused, telling them I wasn't hungry. Truly I was starving, but I felt uncomfortable. I didn't feel truly accepted. Instead, I felt scrutinized like I was under a microscope under constant scrutiny. Everything about me was a curiosity such as, how I used to style my hair, or why I chose to dress in the type of clothing that I used to own.

I was also under heavy surveillance. Everything about me was being watched as if I were going to steal from them. I didn't trust these people with their fake smiles, as much as they didn't trust me. Perhaps I was better off staying at the foster home in Brooklyn. At least I wouldn't feel so scrutinized and judged.

I wanted to walk outside toward the back woods and smoke a joint. I needed to release a lot of tension. As I was about to step outside, Brittney popped into my bedroom. I assumed that she had just taken a shower since she was dressed in a royal- blue bathrobe with white flip flops.

She had a blue towel draped around her neck, which allowed me to see the true texture of her brownish hair. I saw that her roots were just as thick as mine, but straighter at the ends.

"I heard that you were uncooperative today. My mom's thinking about having you sent back," she threatened.

"Please, like I care," I said, sarcastically. "She wouldn't miss me for real anyway."

"I can't believe that you cried over a hair-cut. That's pathetic," Brittney sneered.

"Whatever, you're the one who cried over a fuckin' pair of boots, remember? Now you tell me who's pathetic?"

"You're really embarrassing to look at. You look like one of those dirty African voodoo dolls," Brittney insulted.

"Fuck you! You look like some fake-ass black Barbie who wants to pass!"

My own sister was admitting that she was ashamed to acknowledge me. Instead of hurting my feelings, she made me more defensive.

"Look at me," I said. "I'm your sister and I'm black. You can ignore it all you want. But sooner or later, your roots are gonna catch up to you!" I fired.

"Whatever, you're not my sister. You're probably ones of those black babies that my parents felt sorry for and wanted to take in. You need to go back to your projects for real," Brittney said harshly.

"Bitch!" I yelled, and I slapped her across the face. "What the hell is wrong is with you? We share the same fuckin' blood, for cryin' out loud!"

"Yeah, don't remind me," she said, rolling her eyes in disgust. "I had to draw blood for you the other day."

"What are you talkin' about?" I asked, confused.

"Something about you having a fainting episode. My dad told me all about it," she informed. "He said I would have to give you blood if anything ever happened to you since we're a match."

"Are you for real?" I shrieked.

"Did you really think we had you sent here only because my parents wanted me to have a sister?" she asked with a smirk. "They did it only because they had to based on your medical condition," Brittney explained. "Aren't you anemic?" she asked hatefully.

Ever since I was little, I always struggled with Anemia, but never understood why. I had assumed it was because I was too skinny, which explained why I constantly stayed cold. However I was beginning to realize that I had a blood disorder. But how did she know this? I wondered.

"Don't worry about me. I don't need nothin' from you anyway, sis," I emphasized.

"You're not my sister," Brittney denied.

I soon realized that she wanted to continue convincing herself so that she wouldn't have to acknowledge me.

"Get the fuck outta my face!" I ordered while lighting my blunt.

"Get out of our house."

"You don't have to tell me twice," I replied, now blowing smoke into her face.

"My parents could have you thrown outta here if they knew you had that stuff," Brittney threatened in between coughs.

"Bring it on. You tell your parents I said to kiss my ass, especially to Sylvia," I said, closing my door. I left Brittney standing in the hallway until she huffed and stormed off to tattle to her father.

The next two weeks of my transition were hard. I was expected to behave exactly like my sister. I had to wear her style of clothes, socialize with her friends (who hated me), and attend similar activities with her. Brittney attended modeling classes after school and piano lessons two nights a week. Her swimming lessons were scheduled on weekends, with family day that occurred on Sunday afternoons. I hated the fact that I wasn't allowed to search for my own identity.

I hated playing the piano and struggled with memorizing the music keys. Modeling wasn't an interest for me, since I was self- conscious of my boyish haircut. I was never allowed to bring friends home from school since Sylvia wasn't comfortable around others outside of her elite community. Participating in sports was also not allowed.

There was a time when I wanted to join the girls' basketball and track team. Sylvia mentioned that "those sports" are too urban for our tastes. "We certainly won't have a "girls in the hood" mentality in this household!" she quipped. While at school, Brittney ignored me whenever she saw me between class periods.

If her friends inquired about me, she would start a rumor by saying that I was either a "foreign exchange student or a child they adopted from overseas." She refused to talk to me and her friends would stare at me as though I were covered in dirt.

Soon I became a loner, until I became interested in signing up for the dance club at school. I was extremely excited, since it would provide an opportunity to express internal feelings healthily. "Absolutely not!" Sylvia refused. When I tried to convince David to reconsider, he would behave as though he were afraid of causing an argument with Sylvia.

"You know how your mother feels about these types of things," he'd say sadly. "If she's not happy about it, then let's not upset her."

"I can't believe this shit!" I would cry.

Nothing I did ever pleased them unless I would imitate every action of my so-called, sister who refused to accept me. There were also times when David and Sylvia would have parties or charity events at their home. Whenever friends from their elite circle showed up, I was always asked to remain in closed quarters. As long as I stayed in my room or away from the house during the festivities, Sylvia was happy.

Eventually, I became rebellious by running away or indulging in truancy. Sometimes I would roam different parts of town late at night just to get away. By this time, I had established my own circle of friends, all of whom were minorities. Sonia was African American. Su was from Asia, and Anthony (aka Antoinette) was also African American and a homosexual. I was pleased to have a small peer group, yet none of them ever replaced the close, sisterly bond that Martina and I once shared.

One day she wrote a letter informing me that she was adopted by a religious, middle-aged couple in New Jersey. I couldn't help but laugh to myself, because she would always be a prime example of a promiscuous sinner in a Christian's eye. My rebellious behaviors continued until

Sylvia threatened to send me back to foster care. But David insisted that I should have a second chance.

He was quick to feel sorry for me, yet he wasn't able to defend me with Sylvia. I soon realized that she had control of everything. David didn't have a backbone when it came to dealing with her royal highness. His actions were always weak. He was her puppet on strings. Discussions about my behavior soon led to arguments. Eventually, they realized they could never reshape me into an identical version of their "precious" daughter, Brittney. From then on, I was allowed to participate in activities of my choice, but still had to remain in closed quarters whenever friends came to the house.

"If you're going to stay with us, you'll need to behave more responsibly," David said during dinner one day. "No more skipping school and sneaking out late at night."

Since when did he become so authoritative? I knew that it was Sylvia who put him up to having this discussion.

"Your sister is trying so hard to be a good role model for you," Sylvia added.

The hell she is!

"OK, I can live like a true Kramer family member. But I'm still gonna be me. I can't be the clone of your wonderful daughter, because I have things that I like to do, too," I informed them.

This time, I was ready to restart on the right foot, but wanted to make them aware of my exceptions. What did I have to lose? As time went by, Brittney continued to ignore me in school. She wanted so hard to shut me out of her life.

"She won't be staying with us long. She'll be going back to her country soon," Brittney once told her friends.

"Yes, I will," I would tell myself. "This placement with my so-called family is only a temporary thing until I can leave and be on my own again." From that day forward, I lived with that mentality to help me cope with the feelings of resistance and avoidance that Brittney constantly dished out.

Chapter 8

2004

By the age of 17, I was behaving more maturely and eventually learned to assimilate to the *Kramer culture* by doing whatever pleased them. Now that I was a senior in high school, I began to strive harder toward my future. I still had plans to pursue the medical field. Brittney continued to participate in her extracurricular activities, while I had activities of my own.

She was now a model and performed in local piano recitals. Brittney was also on the girls swim team in school, whereas I joined the girls track team and performed with my dance group at various places throughout the community. Not only was I busy with extracurricular activities but I also maintained a part- time job at a burger joint, Cokey's. Becoming involved in these tasks allowed me to cope and escape from whatever displeased me at home.

There were times when I became resentful that my adoptive parents refused to support me at my dance competitions or track meets. Yet, they were more than eager to attend every one of Brittney's performances and pageants. I couldn't wait to graduate, so that I could finally flee from my unwelcoming environment and live the life I wanted to have. As I continued living with the Kramers, I often tried to maintain independence, whereas my sister constantly relied on her parents for pampering.

Not only was I becoming emotionally mature, but I was also physically fit as well. My hair was now longer and sometimes hung in two-strand twists that fell to my shoulders. At times I would dye my ends a dark auburn to give it a more sultry appearance, or I would sport a crinkly style from a braid-set. By now, I was wearing make-up and had a toned physique, with a washboard stomach and naval piercing.

Occasionally, I still felt inferior, believing that I developed too late. But ironically, I was able to turn heads from all different directions. Boys in school would flirt using their sophomoric lines on me like, "Hey girl, when you gonna let me hit that?" Guys at work would sometimes proposition me for a date, as well as construction workers on the street. Brittney's boyfriends sometimes would make comments as well. We once had a fight about it.

I was in my studio practicing Beyonce and Ciara dance moves when Brittney's boyfriend, Tristan, appeared. I didn't realize that I had an audience until I heard a comment from the doorway.

"Damn, sweet chocolate, you know how to shake that money, don't you?" he cheered.

I turned around, stunned, and stared at him.

"You think you could teach Brittney?" he asked, grinning.

"Thank you," I said, trying to dismiss him. I tried to close the door.

"Why don't you teach me? I could put you in a video," Tristan asked seductively.

I didn't answer. Instead, I gave him a skeptical expression.

"Come on, girl, show me how you shake that," he flirted, placing his hands on my hips. I suddenly felt his manhood begin to rise.

"You need to leave," I resisted, pushing him away.

"But I don't want to. I came for lessons, *mami*," Tristan persisted.

Before I could reply, we suddenly heard Brittney.

"You heard what she said, asshole! Leave her alone!" "And you," she said, now facing me, "put some clothes on, hoochie mama!"

"No bitch, I shouldn't have to. You need to check your man instead!" I fired, standing in her face. I was ready to scrap the way my friends would back in Brooklyn.

I stood facing my opponent as I wore my black leggings and tied-up T-shirt. My hair was pulled up into a French twist.

"Come on, Brittney, I was just kidding," Tristan said, realizing that our fury had escalated. "You know I like to see you dance. I think you'll make a better teacher."

When Brittney wasn't looking, Tristan gave me a wink and I flipped him off and slammed the door in his face. Once they left, I snickered to myself and went back to mimicking the *Bootylicious* dance. Later that night, Brittney and I had another confrontation. She came into my room with a pair of scissors.

"You bitch! Let's see how you wanna dance now!" she yelled.

"You better get the fuck outta here with that shit!" I raged as I hurled my cordless phone at her. She pounced toward me and we began to brawl. As usual, David came to break us apart.

"Come on girls, this is a damn shame. You two are getting too old for these cat fights!" he ordered.

"Yeah, tell me about it," I spat. "You need to check yourself, daddy's girl!" I fired at Brittney.

"You're the one who dresses like a hoochie mama!"

"Shut the hell up, Barbie wanna- be!" I yelled.

"That's enough!" David shouted.

As I began to dress for school, I decided to wear a pair of black *Adidas* sports pants with a matching jacket and halter top. I loved flashing my slim waist and wearing my contour-fitting pants. My hair was down and I sported a pair of sneakers that I had just bought after saving a few of my paychecks. Antoinette had just called, asking me to meet her at the train terminal.

"Hey, Ms. Lady," she greeted. "Meet me in 15 minutes, and hurry girl! You know how those low-down train drivers don't ever wanna wait on us," she warned.

"I'm comin', just hold on!" I said urgently. I was trying my best to hurry as I continued primping myself.

Antoinette knew that I was constantly late to our bus station. David and Sylvia, unfortunately, refused to provide me with a car, but Brittney was given one on her 16th birthday; which was why I had to get up two hours early. I had to scarf down a bowl of *Cap 'n' Crunch* cereal and literally run several blocks for transportation.

"Hey girl!" Antoinette greeted, as we pecked each other on the cheek, once I reached the terminal. "Did you work on some more moves last night?" She was referring to the cho-reographed dances that we had created a week ago.

"Yeah, I'll let you check 'em out when we meet the girls. It's gonna be hot!" I said, excitedly.

"I bet!" Antoinette shrieked.

"I gotta work tonight," I informed.

"Ah man, you always workin'," Antoinette said in disappointment.

"I know it, but I'm all about handlin' my business if you know what I mean."

"I feel ya, girl. A girl's gotta be independent, OK?" she said, flicking her wrist that revealed her acrylic nails. Antoinette knew that I had a plan to leave once I had enough money saved up.

For the rest of the day, I attended classes and stayed after school for track practice. Since I couldn't join my friends for our dance rehearsal at Sonia's house, I rushed straight to work. The minute I stepped inside, I became overwhelmed and anxious. The restaurant was hectic and chaotic.

Customers were hostile due to a long wait to be seated. Our servers scurried around, barely keeping up with their orders, and the cooks shouted across the kitchen, as they were trying to keep up with the pace. Some of the customers shouted at the staff, complaining about not having the right order. A few demanded to have a free meal. Ludacris' new hit *Stand Up* began to rip throughout the blaring speakers.

"Hey Cyndi, come punch in, we really need you!" my manager, Curtis, shouted frantically.

OK, I can do this, I thought. Truly, I was terrified.

Since I didn't get a chance to change into my uniform, I hurried toward the back and slipped into an apron. That night I was assigned to 20 tables without prep, since we were short staffed. I was on the verge of walking out until I heard a soothing voice that I would never forget.

"Calm down, sweetheart, you're doin' a good job."

I turned around and saw the face of a heart-throb. He had a caramel complexion, short, wavy, black hair like Ginuwine, and a trimmed goatee that revealed his sexy smile. Our eyes met and locked hard, as we became speechless.

"Thank you," I said, now becoming bashful.

In the past, I was assertive with men and initiated contact with them. However, with this man, I felt helpless, as if he would take control.

"You're welcome, pretty," he complimented with that smile again.

I continued to blush, now beginning to feel embarrassed, because I nearly dropped his plate of French fries. "Thanks."

"What's your name? Oh don't tell me, it's on your name tag," he said humorously. "Cyndi," he read.

"Yeah."

"I'm Rashad," he extended his hand. "You know you could pass for Lauryn Hill's twin, right? but I suppose you hear that a lot, don't you?"

"Yeah," I answered, still grinning.

Here I was standing in front of him wearing an aerobics outfit. I never had the chance to change out of my dancing attire. No wonder I caught his eye! His eyes began to graze my washboard.

"What time do you get off, Cyndi?"

Before I could answer, I was interrupted by one of my aggravated customers.

"Hey lady, are ya deaf? I'm starving here!" he raged.

"I have to go," I said, urgently.

"What time do you get off?" Rashad repeated.

"Hurry up!" the customer continued.

"I'm really sorry, but I have to go," I apologized, trying to leave Rashad's table.

Unfortunately, he was too quick for me. He suddenly seized my apron and began to smirk. "What time do you get off? Maybe I could hear you sing like Lauryn Hill."

I couldn't believe this guy!

"I have to go!"

"OK, but only if you tell me what time you get off. Otherwise, we can do this all night," he laughed, glancing at his watch.

"Alright, 9:30. Now let me go," I said through clenched teeth.

"Are you sure about that?" Rashad asked, not releasing my apron.

"Yes, now get off me," I said anxiously.

"OK beautiful, I'll see you later," he laughed, finally releasing me.

For the rest of my shift, I forgot about Rashad and continued serving the customers. I didn't expect him to show up. But sure enough on the hour, he pulled up in front of Cokey's in a burgundy SUV.

"What are you doin' here?" I asked the minute I stepped outside.

"I came to take you home. I know you're tired. You worked really hard tonight."

"I really appreciate you comin' out, but I'll be OK," I said, heading toward the train terminal.

"Don't tell me that you're about to walk home," Rashad said, becoming shocked.

"Yeah," I said, becoming sarcastic. "I'm a big girl. Don't worry about me, I got this."

"I supposed that you can fight off hi jackers, too, right?" he asked, snickering.

"Don't worry about me," I said, trying to stifle a laugh.

"I can't help it. A pretty girl like you walkin' around town at odd hours of the night. I would never forgive myself if anything ever happened to you," he said dramatically.

I now began to laugh, realizing that he would debate with me in the parking lot until I agreed, but I did have to admit that my feet and back were killing me.

"So why do you walk home in the middle of the night, Cyndi?" he asked as we drove along the highway.

"My parents didn't supply me with a car last year like they did for my sister."

"You're kiddin', right?" he asked.

"Nooo," I said with a playful pitiful, expression.

"Are you still in high school?" he asked.

"Nah, I'm a freshman now," I lied. "I go to URI."

I wanted to give him the impression that I was older.

"That's what's up! You go to the University of Rhode Island," he said, flashing his sexy smile again.

"What about you?" I asked, now getting the impression that he was a few years older than me.

"No, I had home tutors before I graduated. I was always too busy in the studio, since I practically lived there," he explained.

"The studio? Are you a dancer?" I asked, now impressed.

"No, I'm a model," he answered, smiling.

"Oh, really?"

For the rest of the ride, we talked and told each other about ourselves. I told him of a few incidents from my childhood, leaving out the brutal details of Big Mike. But I mentioned that I was adopted years later. Rashad shared his story, too.

He was 21 and had his own place. His mother raised him as a single parent in Philadelphia, Pennsylvania. Years later, they moved to Boston when he was 15, since his modeling career led them there. Today, he lived in Providence but commuted to Boston for work, since the cost of living was cheaper in Rhode Island. Rashad said his mother started him in modeling when he was just an infant.

"My mother went through hard times when my father left us. He left when I was a year old," Rashad explained. "That was the reason she threw me into TV commercials, so that it could help pay the bills, while she ran a grocery store." He soon began to turn onto my street. For some reason, I didn't want to end our conversation.

"I'm sorry to hear that," I empathized.

"I don't really remember my dad much, but my mom sometimes shares stories about him, if they're not too painful. "Well, here we are, Ms. Lady," he announced, pulling up into my drive way.

"Thank you. I really enjoyed talkin' with you," I said, opening the door.

"I'd like to see you again. I enjoyed talkin' with you, too."

My face became hot again. This was definitely a moment where I could exhale. My heart pounded and my stomach had butterflies fluttering inside. Before I knew it, he was jotting his phone number down on the back of his wallet-sized photo. He told me it was a photo that was taken for a cologne ad. I gave him my phone number and walked toward the house.

"Expect a surprise tomorrow. I want to be sure that I put a smile on that pretty face of yours," he said as he pulled off.

I stood at the front door, hanging onto his every word. What could he have meant when he said to expect a surprise? Before I retreated inside, I stared at his photo again. His teasing eyes reminded me of the male model Tyson with features that appeared partially Asian. His eyes were so dark and piercing.

In his photo, Rashad's seductive smile was alluring, and his toned muscles bulged through his white wife-beater that coordinated with his blue jeans. I began to imagine his scent, as I stared at his advertisement print. From that moment, I was sure that I would have sweet dreams after seeing his smile.

Chapter 9

T he next morning, I received a box of roses at the front door. On the card it read, *Don't walk alone in the dark tonight, because we'll do dinner instead. I'll pick you up at seven. From, Rashad.*

"Who's the new lover boy?" Brittney asked from the hallway, while blow drying her hair.

"Oh, just someone I met at work," I answered, trying to appear nonchalant. Truly, I was ecstatic.

"You can have your little burger-joint job. There's no way in hell I would ever work there," she said in disgust. "I know I wouldn't want to come home smelling like hot grease."

"Whatever, at least I got a job. Plus, I don't have to constantly pretend to be what I'm not!" I fired. I was fed up with this ungrateful chic for sure!

"Gee, what could I possibly be pretending, Cyndi?" Brittney was becoming sarcastic.

"You know what I'm talkin' about. I'm talkin' about you spendin' hours of time slappin' that shit on your hair everyday just so you can blend in with your so-called friends. Who wants to do that shit?" I yelled.

"Well, we'll just see what your lover boy has to say about that! I'm sure he won't complain."

"Whatever, get the fuck outta my face with that shit!" I raged.

I certainly didn't need her to fuck up my glow that I was feeling from Rashad. That guy left a lasting impression on me that I would never forget and I was sick of Brittney always trying to compete with me. She always felt that her lighter complexion and blue eyes would open every door, whereas my darker features would announce me as the outcast. I walked toward my room to dress for school.

For the entire day, I thought of Rashad and only Rashad. He asked *me* on a date and I wasn't sure what to wear or how to style my hair. Maybe I should get a manicure. I remained in a dreamy daze thinking of his smile and soft, kissable lips.

"You're in a chipper mood today. What's up?" Sonia asked, between class periods at school.

"Nothin'," I said, smiling.

"I know that look, girl. Is there something you're not telling me?" she asked. "Let me guess, you got a raise at your job, right?" she began to laugh, imitating a sexual gesture.

"I haven't got a raise yet, but let's just say that I may be gettin' some extensive trainin' real soon," I giggled. "See ya at dance practice!" I scurried off to my next class.

History was my worst class as Mr. Fieldman would put the entire class to sleep with his monotone voice. But today, I was in better spirits. Ironically, I participated in the class discussion and exercise. After school, I attended track practice and dance rehearsal. Because Rashad's gorgeous face remained on my mind, I struggled with keeping up with our group's routine that we'd been practicing for nearly a month. The girls eventually became upset every time I missed a step.

"Cyndi, what's the deal? You know we need to get this move right so we can kill that competition next month," Su complained.

"My bad. Don't worry, I'll get it," I responded, yet still having intense thoughts of Rashad.

"Well, miss thang, you need to get right real soon. 'Cause next month, I'm gonna be all about rippin' that stage," Antoinette said, waving her acrylics in my face.

"Damn! I said I'll get it!" I said sarcastically.

Eventually, I mentally returned and was able to keep up with our steps, which put everyone at ease. Once we finished, I rushed home and searched through my wardrobe for a perfect outfit. I wanted this night to be perfect. When 7:00 struck, I became nervous.

"Your lover boy is here!" Brittney announced from the hallway.

"His name is Rashad," I snapped.

As I walked to the front door, his smile brightened.

"Wow, you're really gorgeous! Are you sure you're not a model?" he asked staring into my eyes.

I giggled like a school girl, which added another spark to his eye.

"I think you should put this in water sweetheart. We certainly don't want to see it wilt," Rashad said, handing me a white rose with a teddy bear.

As I entered the kitchen, David and Sylvia inspected him as though he were a specimen. They scrutinized him and interrogated him with every personal question under the sun. Sylvia inquired about his line of work, work history, where he lived, and level of education. David was intrigued to know about Rashad's personal background.

I knew that Rashad was becoming uncomfortable, since they practically interviewed him as opposed to having a social conversation with him. But he remained polite and gave vague answers to what he was comfortable with discussing. I, on the other hand, became embarrassed and upset. Why did my friends always have to be treated like bugs under a microscope, or stereotyped like common criminals?

"OK, I'm ready!" I announced, ready to leave this awkward moment.

"Have a good time, but don't forget about tomorrow. You have that midterm, remember? " David asked.

"I seriously doubt that midterm exams are gonna be on her mind tonight," Brittney added with a smirk.

"Sure, just like your bio exam wasn't on your mind the other night when you said you went to meet Kailey at the library, right?" I sarcastically asked.

Brittney's face instantly turned beet-red, as she all of a sudden became quiet. She knew that I was referring to a time when she swore up and down to her parents that she went to study with Kailey. But the truth was, that Brittney went to meet Tristan and his friend, Gage, to engage in sexual mischief in their car. I would never forget the time when her parents had a feeling that Brittney's story wasn't adding up, yet she covered her trail so well, they couldn't catch her in a lie.

Before she could add another comment, I left her with her parents as the tension and awkwardness suddenly became thick. Plus, I wanted us to leave before Rashad became suspicious, since David nearly let the cat out of the bag that I was still in high school.

"Bye!" I waved devilishly.

"Damn, are your folks a bunch of investigators? They were really tryin' to grill me like I was tryin' to get up in the White House or somethin'," Rashad laughed as we walked toward his jeep.

"Let's just go," I urged.

We ended up eating at an Italian restaurant called *Vinnie's Pasta*. Once we had our candle- lit meal, we went to an art museum. This was my first date that had a touch of culture and maturity. We talked about our personal goals and dreams that we wanted to pursue.

"I really had a good time," I said.

"I had fun, too. You're pretty cool, Cyndi. A lot of girls I know wouldn't really be into what we did tonight. But, it's all good. Because you're on a totally different level," he said. "Maybe you're on my level," he pulled me toward him and I wanted to melt.

His cologne and gentleness tempted me to ravish him in broad daylight. But instead, I kept my composure. Rashad wasn't the typical teenage thug who strived at getting into my pants with his typical pick-up lines. He was more mature, with a perfect swagger. As he pulled me close, I leaned into him and he kissed me.

His lips were soft and caressing. I let him wrap his strong, toned arms around my waist, as he fed me the passionate affection that I had fantasized about the entire day. We stood outside the museum underneath a gazebo, as the wind caressed our hair and stars shined above us in the night sky. Classical orchestra music began to play a soft melody from inside. Previously, I was more assertive and hostile toward boys. But with Rashad, I couldn't help but let my guard down. I suddenly felt vulnerable and eager to be pursued. From that moment, he had already connected with me.

"I'm really feelin' you, Cyndi. Is there any way I can see you again?"

Why did this night have to end? I thought, now mesmerized.

"Sure," I said, smiling.

He kissed me again and began to carry me to his jeep as though I were his bride.

"I have somethin' that I want to give you," he said. "But only if you promise to always wear it."

"I promise," I pledged dreamily.

Rashad suddenly removed his chain from his neck and placed it around mine. It was a gold chain designed with his name in cursive and enlaced with rhinestone.

"Consider this a special present for a special lady," he said as we kissed.

I wrapped my arms around him and melted in his embrace, returning the affection.

Chapter 10

R ashad and I became closer as two months had passed. By this time, I was successfully juggling school work, dancing, part-time employment and a relationship. Rashad would pick me up from a nearby library on the days that I skipped school and would send special surprises to my home in the mornings. Having him meet me at school would only blow my cover that I wasn't yet a college student.

It was now toward the end of the school year. Students were preparing for graduation and life after high school, including my friends. Antoinette had plans to pursue music choreography in California. She wanted to choreograph dances for R&B artists. Sonia was going to major in fashion design in New York, and Su applied to various volunteer abroad programs. I still had inspirations to become a doctor, but wasn't sure which university to attend.

My best friend, Martina, had recently sent me an e-mail. She had just married an African American in Trenton, New Jersey. She felt it was her only way to get her religious parents to back off with their criticisms of her premarital sex relationship. My adoptive parents had just completed admissions papers for Brittney to attend Harvard next fall.

I knew that she begged them to let her apply, just so she could party and sex her life away. She had always been secretly rebellious, but her parents were always too blind to see it. Brittney was helped by her parents all the way when preparing for college. For me it appeared that I was still the unwanted step-child of the family.

They helped her with completing her college applications and attended freshman orientation with her at the university. Yet, I wasn't given any support or assistance with applying to any universities. At times I resented it, yet on other occasions, I cared less.

"These people aren't my real parents anyway," I would remind myself.

On graduation day, David and Sylvia took off for a summer-long Paris vacation. Once Brittney and I realized we had the entire house to ourselves, she was ready to wreak havoc.

"This is the summer when I can have the time of my life! Whoooh!" Brittney screamed in delight. She began to jump on the living room sofa.

Brittney was ready to be a party animal, whereas I suddenly decided to engage in full-time summer work. She chose to throw wild parties on a daily basis and have neighbors complain or shake their heads in disapproval. Our property soon became a haven for liquor and drugs, within a week. She had different men inside the home every night, along with her arrogant friends, who despised me. Brittney and I often argued about the commotion that she denied was out of control.

"Hey, I'm gettin' tired of this Girls- Gone- Wild act while your triflin' ass is layin' around watchin' me take the rap from your parents!" I fired. "This shit is not cute!"

"Oh, whatever! It's not that serious and besides, I can do whatever I want," she said. "This is my last time that I get to party hard, until I start college in the fall."

I stood in front of my sister and fought the urge to smack her. Instead, I tried to remain stable.

"This isn't even your house anyway," Brittney continued. "My parents only took you in because they felt sorry for you. They didn't do it out of *love*," she emphasized, rolling her eyes. "Please tell me you knew that."

I wanted to cry. I couldn't believe she was saying this to me!

"Well, you won't have to worry about me much longer. I'll be outta here real soon. Trust and believe that!"

"Oh you can bet that I will. Get the hell out!"

"You can forget about me savin' your triflin' ass when your rich- ass parents get back!" I cried.

I stormed into my room and began to pack a bag. I ended up going to Rashad's, where I could be loved and treated like a queen like I deserved to be.

Rashad was concerned the minute I walked through the door. "What's wrong, sweet- heart?" he asked. He closed the door behind him.

"I hate her! I can't stand her ass!" I cried, stomping though his apartment. I slammed my bag down and cried hot, angry tears.

"Who are you talkin' about, sweetheart? Calm down," he soothed, now following me toward his living room.

"Who else could I be talkin' about? My very own sister who has hated me from day one. She's never wanted me around from the day my parents signed on the dotted line and made my adoption final," I explained.

"Well, the hell with her!" I raged. "We don't have to acknowledge each other as sisters. I don't really give a fuck!"

"Calm down, Cyndi."

I continued to cry, which eventually led to heavy sobs. My eyes became swollen, my throat began to hurt, and my chest ached. I was emotionally exhausted from the mental anguish that had gone on long enough.

"Come on, Cyndi, you're makin' yourself sick. I don't like to see you like this," Rashad said. Tears had now formed in his eyes.

"Why the hell are you cryin'?" I asked in between sobs.

"Because you're hurtin'. When I see that you're hurtin', I feel your pain, too."

I clung to him and continued to cry until his shoulder became soaked. When I had arrived so upset, I hadn't noticed that my outburst had interrupted his shower. His towel clung to his soaked body, and his wavy hair was still dripping. But I saw that it was brushed neatly in place, and his body exuded his signature cologne that I loved. Although I had been upset, I suddenly became excited. Rashad had a body that was similar to the music artist D'Angelo in his video, *How Does it Feel*. I nearly salivated when I glanced at his toned, muscles that lead to his indentation.

"Oh, sorry," I said, now trying to be modest as I looked at his attire over.

"It's OK. I was about to get dressed anyway," he said.

"Well, I'll let you finish gettin' dressed. We were supposed to go out anyway," I started to pull away.

"Nah, I changed my mind. Come here, baby," he said seductively.

"Why?"

He acted as though he didn't hear me. Rashad stood in the living room, drawing me closer toward him. He gazed into my eyes for the longest time. I suddenly became lost in his eyes and was speechless.

"Just come here," he repeated, now leading me toward his bedroom.

Once we were in his room, he began to kiss my neck, as he gently removed the straps of my sundress from my shoulders. I let it fall to the red carpeted floor and became his vulnerable lover. Rashad immediately unwrapped his towel and let it fall. He wiped a tear from my eye and softly kissed my forehead to my nose and eventually to my lips.

I let him remove my push-up bra that accentuated my cleavage, still caught up in his romantic swagger. Rashad always had this affect on me. He took off the chain from around my neck that he had once given me, and tossed it onto the dresser.

I suddenly came back to my senses. I finally spoke up. "Rashad, we shouldn't. Not yet."

"Baby, don't worry, I know what I'm doin'. Just trust me," he said, staring into my eyes.

Rashad knew what I was referring to. Many times we had discussed waiting until I visited the clinic to be put on a contraceptive. He had suggested that we attend the appointment together, so that my first time could be special.

Ever since I was 13, I had always fantasized about my first time. I used to imagine who my lover would be whether it would be a beautiful experience, or one that I would regret. I had overheard some of the girls in the gym locker-room discuss their experiences, which made me feel as though I had matured too late. I didn't have anything in common with those girls, since they had indulged in sex much earlier than me.

I became nervous. Anticipation grew and he sensed it. "You're my girl, Cyndi. I wanna be with you," he said. "Do you trust me?"

"Yeah."

He kissed me again and picked me up as I wrapped my legs around his waist. I let him carry me to his king-size bed. As he laid me down, Rashad began to kiss me in places no man had ever been before. I let him remove my black, lacy underwear with his teeth and began to melt under his creative foreplay.

I tried to return to my senses. I reached for his nightstand beside the bed, hoping that I could find a condom. But he gently seized my hand and slipped his fingers into mine as he quickly hovered over me.

"Rashad, we need to use somethin'," I whispered as I closed my eyes. His lips traveled down my breasts toward my stomach. Soon, he returned to my valley and began to explore between my thighs, as tears of pleasure came into my eyes. My eyes remained closed, but I felt what was happening. Instantly, my womanhood became his precious canvas to paint. My body cringed, as his tongue became the paintbrush. He painted large and heavy strokes, hitting every crevice.

Then, I felt him enter me for the first time. I initially cringed from the pain. My goodness, he was blessed! More kisses returned to my neck and shoulders as his pace increased. "I'll put one on next time. I promise," he weakly said in my ear.

Rashad's passion that once started as slow and gentle soon increased and became exotically rough. I dug my nails in his back as, he continued to thrust harder. My arms wrapped tightly around his broad shoulders and he exploded in ecstasy.

"Damn, baby!" I cried.

"Oh shit!" Rashad gasped. I felt his body tense and jerk as he buried his face in my neck. Once our love making ended, we slept for a few hours, watching the afternoon sky become dark.

At 9:00 p.m., I became hungry and strutted into his kitchen to heat up a microwave dinner. We had missed our dinner reservation a few hours ago. His apartment was dark and I was still nude from our rumple in the sheets. I had wanted to bring in our food on a TV tray, so that we could eat in bed. Instead, Rashad beat me to it.

I felt him sneak up behind me and slam me down on the counter, taking me from behind. I held onto the counter top and tried to hold back my explosion. When I thought he was finished, he turned me around toward him and picked me up, as we headed toward the hallway. I let him slip his strong, toned arms underneath my thighs and press me up against the wall. As I held onto him, he took me on another wild, exotic adventure. My eyes became teary as his penetrations pushed deep.

Once our wild ride ended, we slipped into the shower to finish another round. Soap suds ran down his chest as he caressed my breasts. Rashad surprised me with multiple positions as hot water rained on us and the room became steamy. He took me from behind again, and then shortly afterwards allowed me to straddle him as he held onto my shoulders. After our shower, Rashad laid me down on his bed and massaged me with baby oil. Once he had finished, I laid on his chest and let him caress my back as I inhaled the sweet scent of his cologne.

For the rest of the summer, I stayed with Rashad, while Brittney continued to throw wild parties at home. I wanted to avoid running into her, in fear that we would have another confrontation. Instead, I ended up working full-time at Cokey's. Most of my friends had already applied for jobs or traveled on a summer vacation, which allowed me more opportunities to lay with Rashad.

This picture- perfect arrangement was short lived when I discovered I was three months pregnant. I slept a lot and experienced crying spells. Morning sickness was also brutal, which created more panic. I didn't want to tell Rashad until I was completely sure. There was a time when I threw up in the restroom at work and one of my co-workers, Heather, overheard me as she came in to wash her hands.

"I'm really scared. I don't know what to do," I sobbed.

"The signs are definitely there, but have you taken a test yet?" she asked.

"No," I sniffled.

"Go buy a pregnancy test as soon as you leave here and see your doctor first thing in the morning. It's important that you have a chance to explore your options," Heather advised.

"Oh my God!" I cried.

"Have you told your boyfriend yet?" she asked.

"No."

"If you are, you gotta tell him sooner or later," she said, hugging me.

Heather encouraged me to call in for sick, so that I could do exactly what she advised. Since I was still in denial, I bought two tests, hoping that the results would be negative for both.

As I followed the instructions on the box, I didn't even have to wait for the results to appear. I saw a pink line emerge immediately, before I could set it down. "Damn!"

"I'm home, sweet heart!" Rashad announced as he came in. He had just returned from his photo shoot. "How's my wifey doin'?"

"I got a surprise for you, too," he said, kissing me, once he walked into the living room.

"We need to talk."

Rashad began to ramble about how his photo shoot went, giving me every detail of what happened. I couldn't get a word in, since he was so excited, until I blurted my news.

"Rashad, I'm pregnant."

"What!" he suddenly stopped and stared at me speechless. "Wait a minute. Tell me I didn't hear what I think I heard."

"You think I'm makin' this shit up? I'm scared too. I don't know what to do!" I cried.

"You better go handle that shit. I'm not dealin' with this. Not at a time like this," he scoffed.

I couldn't believe what I was hearing. How could his mannerism change so instantly?

"I think it's too late for that," I said.

"I'm not goin' for this Cyndi. I know you're not about to trap me. Hell, no!"

"I told you we should've used somethin'!" I yelled. "What were your words? Trust me, Cyndi. I know what I'm doin'. I promise I'll use a condom next time," I imitated. "Well that next time never happened!"

"Look, this shit is crazy. I can't be with you if you don't take care of it. That's the truth," he stated. "I'm at the peak of my career and I'm not about to let some situation pull me down."

"Rashad, please don't say that," I begged.

"You tell me what I'm supposed to do. What the hell am I supposed to do with a baby!" he yelled.

"A few minutes ago, you just called me your wifey. We can work through this," I pleaded. I knew there was no hope in holding onto him at that point, but I didn't want to let him go.

"The hell we can. I'm tellin' you, Cyndi, you either take care of it, or we're done!"

"I can't!" I cried in tears.

"Well, damn, there's always adoption."

"Fuck that!" I shouted.

"Why?" he demanded.

"Because I came up in the system. There's no way in hell I would ever put my child through that. Not after all the shit I went through," I explained.

"I don't know what else to tell you, Cyndi. We're done!"

"Rashad, I know you don't mean that. Just know that you'll always have one thing from me." In my heart, I was hoping that I could keep him.

"And what's that?"

"I love you," I said, desperately.

"That's not gonna pay my bills and I don't have time for this," he started to walk out.

"Rashad, don't go!" I grabbed his arm.

He snatched away abruptly, which made my heart ache excruciatingly.

"Please!" I cried.

As he headed toward the door, I clung to him, hoping that I could keep him from walking out. But deep inside, I knew that I was fooling myself.

"We're done, Cyndi. It's over," he shoved me to the floor.

I couldn't move. I wanted to die.

"The next time you see me, keep it movin', 'cause that's what I'll always be doin' whenever I see you," he slammed the door behind him.

"Rashad! Rashad!"

I wanted him to spin around and rush through the door with tons of apologies and lots of affection, like he always provided. But instead, I only heard the sound of his footsteps drift further away. After remaining on the floor until I could no longer cry, I rose and began to pack my belongings. My mission was to now return to my other home that never welcomed me. Rashad was never going to come back into my life.

Chapter 11

The minute I arrived home, I went straight to bed. I walked past Brittney's party mess and trash that she had accumulated from entertaining for the past three months. Dirty dishes with crud were scattered on the tables, and so much food and empty beer bottles covered the floor that I nearly stumbled. I found a few used condoms and piles of clothing scattered throughout the living room. I saw that some of her favorite CDs and DVDs were mixed into the sloppiness, and the TV flickered.

The living room furniture had dried food stains and several ripped cushions. Brittney was nowhere in sight, but I continued toward my room and collapsed onto my bed to cry myself to sleep. My intention was to nap for an hour, but apparently I had slept the entire day, because when I woke up I realized that my room was dark and a crowd of people scurried around noisily outside my bedroom.

"Just go ahead and steam clean it so that my parents will never suspect anything," I heard Brittney order.

"Right away, Ms. Kramer," they complied.

I soon heard steam cleaners fire and furniture move about. The house became busy and boisterous. *Surely* she couldn't be doin' what I think she's doin'? I thought.

As soon as I opened my bedroom door, I realized that my sister had hired a cleaning service to cover her trail of craziness from the summer. Her orders were so abrupt and sharp that the staff became nervous while cleaning.

"Come on, guys, I'm paying you all top dollar to get this place cleaned. What the hell is so hard about that?" she demanded, while dripping orange Popsicle juice on her parents' white suede furniture.

"You're really pathetic, you know that?" I sneered.

If her parents only knew that she constantly put on a front for them.

"Oh, you're back," she said, realizing that I entered the living room. "Where have you been all this time?"

"Don't worry about me," I snapped.

As the cleaning company continued to steam clean, I went to surf on the Internet in my room since I was bored. Since David was the most reputable attorney in his community, the Internet had articles about all his success stories in the court room. Most of them were about criminal cases and a few discussed custody battles.

There once was a time when he and Sylvia had a cocktail party at their home. Lots of guests attended and socialized in the backyard. As David and Sylvia mingled with their rich friends, I hacked into David's system and read summaries of his cases. I knew that I didn't have a chance of being caught, because as long as I stayed out of David and Sylvia's way during a gathering, they were happy. Rather than allowing me to socialize with others, I kept myself entertained with TV or the Internet, which gave me full advantage of searching his hard drive.

David had copies of archived cases from 10 years ago. Some were about surrogate parents who fought to have full custody of their children. Others had stories about DNA cases. But in this case, I decided to read some of his current cases that dealt with adoption.

At first I came across a story about a girl who discovered her biological parents after 15 years. During early childhood, she was raised believing that her parents were fugitives. They left her under a bridge along a highway and headed off to hide from the law. Years later, she discovered they were institutionalized. Toward the end of the report, I read how the family eventually reunited after experiencing a dispute in the court room. As I was about to log off the computer, I suddenly came across an archived folder labeled *Custody Battle of 1987.*

Part of me now wanted to close out of the system, yet I was intrigued. As I opened the file, I came across more folders that were chronologically organized by month and year. At this point, I felt as though another being had taken control of my body. I suddenly found myself staring at a report that had my birth date on it. As I read it, I soon regretted what I discovered. On the monitor, I had answers to every question that I had my entire life. It read:

At approximately 2:30 a.m. Ciandra Latrice Taylor was delivered February 16, 1987, in Atlantic City, New Jersey. Her mother, Shalana Taylor, at the age of 18, gave birth, after attempting to escape from the Greenville Women's Correctional Facility. A civilian, identified as a truck driver, was found trying to help her escape, but failed when law enforcement caught up with him. Shalana Taylor was immediately transported back to the correctional facility once she was captured.

Immediately after delivery, the infant Ciandra, was taken from the mother and was placed into foster care in Burlington, New Jersey. The mother had been charged with a drug conviction and was sentenced to 14 years in the Greenville Women's Correctional Facility. In 1990 at the age of 3, Ciandra was removed from her foster home due to neglect and was placed in a second home in New York, New York. No contact with the mother was established. In 1992, at the age of 5, Ciandra was removed from the foster home due to reported physical abuse and was sent to a group home in Brooklyn, New York. She resided in the group home for several years until 1999.

At the age of 12 in 1999, Ciandra experienced a fainting episode, when police officers discovered her at a park after witnessing the scene of a shoot- out. Paramedics transported her to St. Michael's Children's Hospital for treatment and observation. After discharge, Ciandra was adopted and placed in the care of David and Sylvia Kramer. The adoption was finalized in Providence, Rhode Island.

No contact has yet been established with the biological mother. She has been transferred to another correctional facility. No information has been released on the new location and clinicians have struggled to obtain records of her current status. Information on the biological father has not been released.

The minute I finished reading about my dreadful past, I sat at my desk and cried. All my life I have lived a lie. Why? I still had many questions that needed to be answered. Earlier, I had regretted that I was carrying Rashad's child. He was persistent in terminating the pregnancy. But somehow, I now had second thoughts.

My mind was made up and I knew exactly what I needed to do. I quickly printed the report and closed out of the system. Brittney busted in the minute I finished.

"Can't you knock?" I fired.

"Mom and dad are back. They want to see us," she informed, ignoring my irritated tone. "Boy, you look a mess. What happened to you?" she laughed.

"Get the fuck out!" I threw a book at her, but missed.

"What's your problem? PMS?"

Before I could answer, she closed the door.

"Hey dad! How was your trip?" she chirped as she entered the living room.

I sat in my room and mimicked her in disgust, realizing that not only did I hate her, but that I was envious. Brittney had a father who was proud to spoil her until the day she died. I, on the other hand, had a father who had been missing for over a decade. And now my child was going to go without a father. Somehow, it seemed as though history had a way of repeating itself with me.

"Well, hello ladies. How have my two favorite girls been getting along?" David asked as he sat his luggage down.

He stood at the front door beaming as if we both just won a medal.

"We survived," Brittney answered with her false charm.

"Oh, if you only knew," I said, wanting to punch her in the face.

Sylvia began to whine and complain, which made me want to choke her. How could they all walk around like sunshine, knowing that other people around them were miserable?

"Oh, Brittney, you haven't been keeping up with your hair," she said dreadfully.

Sylvia stood beside David with her carry-on bag across her shoulder. Both of them were dressed in matching tennis outfits.

"Sorry, mom, I've been busy," she said.

"Oh, she's been busy alright," I stated sarcastically.

"And you haven't been keeping up with your nails either. Brittney, what have you been doing all this time?" Sylvia asked in disappointment.

"Do you really wanna know?" I asked.

For some reason, everyone was ignoring me.

"I said I was sorry! Daddy, do something," Brittney whined.

I stood in the hallway and rolled my eyes. All three of them were making me sick to my stomach.

"OK, I'm sure all this can be resolved. Why don't we all sit down so that we can catch up," David suggested. "I want to hear about your summer."

I could tell that he wanted to change the subject. Being around these two broads was torture.

"I had a really good time," Brittney began. "I hung out with Kailey and Meagan."

"There's somethin' that I wanna talk about," I said. "I wanna talk about why..."

"You know, it's time that we schedule your facial. How about we call them tomorrow?" Sylvia interrupted.

I was ready to announce the discovery that I had just found, yet nobody wanted to pay attention to what I had to say for some reason.

"I can see that you're starting to get pimples. Maybe you weren't drinking enough water," Sylvia continued.

I suddenly began to laugh hysterically. For once, Sylvia discovered a flaw with her daughter. I never thought I would live to see the day.

"What the hell are you laughing at?" Brittney demanded.

I stared at her and snickered.

"What the hell is so funny, fatty?" she added. "Have you taken a look in the mirror lately? You might wanna join the gym."

I realized that she was referring to my water retention that was now beginning to show. "Whatever," I said. "I may have a big-ass stomach, but at least I can hide that. But havin' acne, that's somethin' that you gotta deal with as other people see how ugly you are."

"God, I hate you!" she fired.

"Well you can believe that I never cared much for your fake ass either!"

"Girls!" Sylvia yelled in shock.

"Hey, you know what?" Brittney said, sarcastically. "There's times when I think we're not even related. Sometimes I wonder if maybe the doctors switched you at birth. I mean, look at you. You don't look *anything* like me!"

"That's too bad for your *real* sister, right?" I smarted off. "Or maybe, *you* were switched at birth. Have you ever thought of that? Maybe that explains why you're so triflin'. I bet you had a mom who was a straight up'ho!"

"Girls, stop it!" David yelled, becoming furious. "I've never seen two sisters hate each other so much. It's sad."

"She's not my sister," Brittney said.

"Don't say that. You two may need each other one day," David warned.

"Please," Brittney replied, rolling her eyes.

"I won't need her. I'd rather go homeless than live with her!" I yelled. Tears began to stream down my cheeks.

My sister and I were just never meant to get along.

"That's the best thing that I've ever heard you say," Brittney smirked.

"Good, I'm glad I made your day!"

This time I rose from my seat. I was ready to go blow to blow with her. It was time to give her an ass beating that was long overdue.

"Both of you, just stop!" David fired, now rising.

He stood between us trying to calm our confrontation.

"Get the fuck outta my way!" I cried at David.

"Get out of our house. We never wanted you. Tell her, Sylvia!" Brittney yelled.

"Brittney, please stop," Sylvia pleaded.

There was no stopping us. Brittney and I were ready to go to war. All of our built up hatred that we carried for five years was now ready to be released. David tried to restrain me as Sylvia restrained Brittney. No matter what they said, my sister and I wanted to claw each other's eyes out.

Once we became calm, David released me and I sat down. Sylvia still continued to seize Brittney.

"Get a hold of yourselves, please!" David ordered.

"You know what? I'm sick of this shit! I'm done!" I was fed up.

I tried to approach Brittney to have a civilized conversation with her. "I don't wanna fight with you anymore, Brittney," I said.

I expected her to become remorseful and turn the other cheek. But instead, she became vicious again.

"Go back to your slummy foster home, where you came from!"

I suddenly slapped her and she grabbed my hair. I kicked her legs as hard as I could. Our war-zone became intense as we scuffled and broke the living room table. She ended up ripping my shirt and I scratched her face.

"Go back to the projects, bitch!" she yelled.

As we fought, we ended up near the stairway, where I suddenly lost my balance. I felt myself tumble down the long staircase until my face finally met the tile.

"Oh my God!" Sylvia cried.

"Cyndi!" David cried, running down the stairs.

I was in too much pain to move. All I could do was lay there and moan until I blacked out. The next thing I remember was lying on a stretcher inside the paramedics' vehicle. I felt myself slip in and out of consciousness as my head and body ached. The sirens blared in my ears and the bright neon flashers enhanced my headache. Feeling excruciating pain, I cried silently, fearing that I may die. The paramedics rushed me to the emergency room, where nurses connected me to various tubes and an IV. I felt like a specimen, with so many tubes in me.

"Stay with me, Cyndi! Please stay with me!" I heard a nurse shout.

I tried to fight the darkness that wanted to take over my body. Maybe I was facing death. But I couldn't fight. I didn't have the strength. I tried to glance around to see if I could recognize anyone familiar. Instead, all I could see was a blur of blood, which sent me into panic. I saw bruised welts on my arms and felt blood streaming down the side of my face.

I heard a monitor flat-line to a slower pace, which I soon realized was my heartbeat barely making it. As I felt myself slipping into blackness, I suddenly found myself standing inside an open pasture. I saw an open field lined by tall trees. A stream of water was in front of me, which looked inviting. I saw two children standing on the opposite side of the stream, staring at me. One of them reached out toward me whereas the other did not. I soon became confused, not understanding what was happening. Behind me was a beam of light, which I assumed led back to the physical world; since I stood at a crossroad between life and death.

As I stood in the pasture, I heard activity from the beaming light that sounded as though a team was cheering. The distant sound appeared and was difficult to hear clearly. But I had a feeling they were cheering for me to remain with them. Still feeling confused, I wasn't sure whether I should go forward or retreat in the opposite direction. Eventually one of the children at the stream began to drift away, but left the other standing at the stream. I couldn't make out the gender since the figure was dressed in a gown similar to an angel. But for some reason, I had the impression this was my child.

I started to approach the figure until it became distant. Each time I edged closer toward it, the image would slowly drift further away, which made it difficult to reach. Once the figure disappeared, I began to think of how my child would need me. The world was cruel and people were so evil. There was no way I would ever let anything harm my child similar to how I had been treated while growing up. My child would always be loved.

As I came to this realization, a spark of inner strength soon emerged and I was ready to return. Something indicated that I didn't have much time left, because the cheering in the distant light became clearer. They were extremely urgent and anxious to see me survive. I turned toward the light and ran as fast as I could, hoping that I could race back into the physical world in time. As I approached the light, I saw the team of nurses who struggled to revive my flat-lined heart beat. I raced toward them and soon found myself lying in the hospital room.

As my eyelids flickered, I heard a nurse calling my name and the monitor's rhythm began to increase. "Come on Cyndi! Come on!" she yelled.

Once my vitals were stable, I heard a physician enter the room. Maybe he had good news for me.

"We thought we lost you, but you made it," he said, smiling.

"What happened to me?" I asked, trying to make sense of what occurred. I knew that my experience would be unexplainable.

"You suffered a blow to the head and a concussion. But I know that you're going to get through this," he explained. "Do you want to tell me what happened at home?"

I wanted to answer, but for some reason, my concern wasn't about myself anymore. I wanted to know if I had miscarried.

"Am I still pregnant?" I asked.

"Let's talk about you first," he suggested.

Chapter 12

The doctors wanted me to remain in the hospital for a week for more treatment and observation. Unfortunately, I suffered a sprained arm and a few stitches on the side of my face. But luckily, the injury didn't affect my pregnancy. The doctors were concerned, when I had flat lined that they weren't going to be able to revive me. Of course, I knew that I had experienced a miracle toward the end.

"OK, Cyndi, it would be helpful if you just told us everything that happened from the beginning," an investigator informed.

Now that I had recovered from flat-lining, a social worker was required to report my injury, since it was domestic assault.

"I don't wanna talk about it," I refused, sinking back into my hospital bed.

"We're here to help you, Cyndi. You know that, don't you?"

At first I refused to disclose the incident. I didn't truly trust this officer. But after shedding tears, I eventually became weak and described every detail of how the fight at home began. I mentioned how Brittney and I were at each others' throats and that arguments were always intense, now remembering that Brittney pushed me down the stairs. Once

Cyndi

I gave my statement, the officer left and headed toward my home to take a statement from my parents.

Brittney, unfortunately, wasn't charged with physical assault since her father had the money and power to protect her from the law. Rather than sending her to a cell, she was sent off to an anger management program for six weeks. After sitting around a campfire expressing her feelings with a bunch of rich, troubled teens, her record would somehow disappear, so that she could enter her first semester of college with a fresh start.

How I hated our crooked system with our privileged people! David was a reputable attorney who had enough money and knew important people. He always had the power to sweep his dirty secrets under the rug and live without a conscious.

As I thought of my situation, I became angry. I realized that David and Sylvia played a role as my parents only on paper. They provided me food and shelter during the last five years. But I never received affection. I wasn't offered the opportunities that Brittney had the advantage to have. I was truly the unwanted daughter. David would do whatever he could to protect his perfect image that he wanted to maintain, rather than care for my medical needs. Another predicament that haunted me was my unplanned pregnancy.

Part of me wanted to pursue taking Rashad to court for child support since he didn't want to be involved. But I also knew that I would open another can of worms since I was under 18. Rashad had the impression that I was a year older since I had lied about my age when we first met. So if he was sent off to jail, I knew that I would suffer without his financial support.

What can I do? I asked myself sadly.

"Well, I must say, we didn't expect you to be in this situation. For some reason, I had always anticipated this would happen with Brittney," Sylvia commented with a smirk once I was discharged. We sat in the living room to have our so-called family meeting.

"And so you have it. I'm the one who's fucked, and not your sweet, precious daughter," I spat. "I bet this just makes your day, huh?"

"Cyndi," David, interrupted, trying to break the tension. "We had no idea that you were pregnant."

"What are you going to do?" Sylvia asked.

"What the hell can I do? I have to deal with it," I insisted.

"Are you serious? Come on, let's be realistic here. You're only 17. You have a high school education and that's it," she said. "What do you have to offer this poor child?"

"I'll do whatever I have to do," I answered.

"That's certainly not gonna pay the bills when your child comes. You're a smart girl, use your head," she snapped.

"Yeah, money's important, but damn, is that all you think about? Money, clothes, credit cards and fancy spas? No wonder Brittney came out the way she did!" I yelled.

"I think what we're trying to say is that we were hoping that you had plans for yourself," David explained. "Why jeopardize all that now?"

"Oh, like you really care! It's not like you two had me enrolled to attend Harvard with Brittney!"

"Then what is your plan?" Sylvia asked.

"I'm goin' to Spelman."

"You're kidding, right?" Sylvia said on the verge of laughter.

"What the hell is wrong with you!" I cried.

"Do you honestly think you can do that? With a child? Who's going to pay for your application fees? What about tuition? Oh, let me guess, you're putting that on childcare expenses, right?" Sylvia asked, humorously.

It was obvious that she wanted to mock me rather than support me. Why was I talking with this lady?

"It's obvious that you don't wanna help me. Did you even want to encourage me to go to college?" I asked.

Sylvia didn't answer. Instead, she returned a cold stare that told me enough.

"I didn't think so!" I raged. "Don't worry about me, I'll be fine."

I was now on the verge of tears. They never supported me in anything that I wanted to do. Nor did they ever take the time to learn about the things I enjoyed. I was always shuffled aside or ignored. For once I wanted to do something for myself. Why couldn't I get support with what I wanted to do?

"Really, Cyndi, do you think that's attractive? A young black mother on public assistance with no father. Let's use common sense here. Think about it," Sylvia said.

"Oh, I've thought about it. And like I said, don't worry about me. You never cared much for me anyway. So why are you full of advice now?"

"You're right, because if you think we're going to support you now, think again," she stated coldly. "I'm certainly not up to facing this situation again."

What did she mean by that last statement? I wondered.

"Whatever, I'm outta here," I started to rise.

"Do you really want to become a statistic, Cyndi?" David asked.

I walked toward my room and blocked out his comment.

As soon as I closed my bedroom door, I sat on my bed and reviewed everything that had occurred in my life. I thought about good and bad memories of living in Brooklyn, and I thought of my best friend, Martina. I remembered seeing Taj's smile that used to make me laugh, and I had memories of wreaking havoc with Ms. Francis when she would struggle to catch me. I also began to think of Rashad, remembering the first night we met. Then I thought of Brittney. It was a shame that we couldn't love each other as true sisters. After processing different feelings, I got up and began to pack a bag.

I didn't bother folding any of my clothes. Instead, I threw in T-shirts, jeans, socks, underwear, and the necklace and teddy bear that Rashad had given me. I grabbed his photo and shoved it inside the bag. At first, I wasn't sure where I wanted to go. Too much impulsiveness had clouded my judgment. That is, until I suddenly spotted the printed information about my mother. I snatched the paper, grabbed my bag, and stormed out.

"There's somethin' that I need to know!" I ordered at David.

Sylvia had just gone to bed.

"Cyndi, don't go," he pleaded, as he recognized my packed bag. "We can get through this some kinda way. This is your home too."

"No, this isn't my home! My home is with my mother who I never got to have," I said, defensively.

"I understand exactly how you feel, sweetie. Your mother's dead," he said, sadly.

"No the fuck she's not!"

"Cyndi, please get a hold of yourself. She's gone."

"How can you sit there and lie to me like that? You tell me the truth now, or I swear I will blow your cover to the press!" I threatened.

"There's nothing to report, Cyndi. Your mother's gone and there's nothing we can do about it but accept it."

"You sure about that?" I asked, giving him one final time to confess.

"Of course."

"Whatever. How do you fuckin' explain this then?" I waved the printed information in front of him.

"What do you have?"

"Take a look and see for yourself!" I fired.

He glanced at it, at first trying to dismiss it until I shoved the document closer in his face. David glared at the paper until his eyes became large.

"Where did you get this?" he asked, now becoming teary- eyed.

"Don't worry about how I got it. You just tell me the truth. You owe me that!"

"OK, you really wanna know? Maybe it's time that you're told. You're a big girl now," he said, becoming stern. "Sit down."

I slowly sat across from him in the recliner and dreaded the horrid news that could possibly haunt me forever. My heart began to race and my palms became sweaty. But I was ready to learn about my past to help prepare myself for whatever was in store in my future.

Chapter 13

I sat across from David and listened intently as he began to describe the details of my ugly past. "When I first met your mother, I was captivated by her beauty and that Trina and Lil' Kim rough-around-the-edges persona of hers," he said, snickering.

"Your mother had the most flawless, co-coa complexion and innocent brown eyes. I loved her smile. That was always something that made me weak. In fact, there's a lot of times when I see her in you," David, said continuing to reminisce.

"You have her bone structure, her mannerisms, and that quick temper of hers. But anyway, her name was Shalana, but everyone called her Mocha. It fit her so well."

"That was the name that she wanted to use for her stage name, too. Your mother was a dancer, and boy could she put on a show! She had incredible moves on that stage!" David tried to smile through his tears.

"I like to dance too," I said, now wishing that she could see my given talent.

"It was a Friday night," he continued.

"I went to a club to have a drink with a couple of my buddies. It was one of those nights when we needed to blow off some steam since the bar exam was so intense.

"But when I saw your mother on that stage, I fell in love. She was beautiful. I was so mesmerized by her body, it was crazy. I had to talk to her. And I did. After her performance, I had one of my friends ask the manager to let us have a private show with Mocha.

"She gave me a special performance and started to leave with a huge tip until I gave her one of my business cards. I didn't expect your mother to call me, but she did.

"We hit it off so well that we called each other every night. Shalana meant the world to me. I really wanted to marry her. Everything was perfect. We moved into an apartment and tried to build a life together. She gave up her dancing and I took care of everything. But we had a problem that always gnawed at our side.

"I was married. Sylvia and I were having our differences during that time. We were on two different wave-lengths, and I loved Shalana. She was my world. Before we knew it, Shalana was pregnant with Brittney, and I was caught in a battle.

"I was stuck in a marriage that was going nowhere, but living with a lover who was so full of fire. She was also the mother of my child. I really loved her, but I was confused.

"It wasn't long until Brittney was born and more problems occurred. Your mother began to have a fling with another man, since I apparently couldn't give her all the love and attention that she needed. He was an older guy from Jamaica and I resented him.

"She continued to date her lover and I was still married to Sylvia. We fought like cats and dogs about it so much that she gave me an ultimatum. Shalana told me that she would end her fling with her lover if I divorced Sylvia. But I couldn't do that. That broke your mother's heart. She cried many times.

"Instead of ending her relationship with her Jamaican lover, Shalana became pregnant with you. Now that I was trapped in a love triangle with two children involved, our problems went from bad to worse.

"Here I was a man who lived dual roles. I was married to a judge's daughter, and rendezvousing with an exotic dancer who mothered my child and already had one of her own. Just imagine how I would've been perceived.

"During that time, I was trying to get into law school. I realized that I had to clean up my image. Sylvia didn't have a clue about Shalana, and Shalana was waiting to see where we stood in our relationship.

"I woke up every morning at home, pretending to be the faithful husband. But then I also stayed a few nights with Shalana, trying to be a family man. A few weeks before your conception, Brittney was just learning to walk. This was when I announced to your mother that our relationship was over. I decided to stay married to Sylvia, but wanted to take Brittney with me."

"Your mother cried and fought me. She couldn't understand that I was making this decision for the best interest of all of us. I left your mother inside the apartment as she cried. She sat at the front door and screamed as I walked away with Brittney.

"Internally, I was torn apart as much as she was, but I couldn't let her see it. It was a hard decision to make, but it was for the best. I can still hear her cries today. There's not a day that goes by that now has me feeling remorseful," David concluded, finishing his story.

I sat in disbelief until anger built up.

"So, you did all that just to cover your ass, right?" I accused.

"Please don't think of it that way," he said remorsefully.

"Whatever," I muttered. "You just wanted to cover your ass so that you wouldn't fuck up your prestigious image!"

I continued to yell at him, which made David cower in his seat.

"You couldn't face up to your responsibilities and accept that you secretly indulged in an affair with a black, exotic dancer and had a bi-racial child. What an asshole! So, typical!" I was disgusted.

"If you really loved my mother like you said, you would've done the right thing and faced up to your responsibilities of takin' care of us. But you didn't. You only looked out for yourself!"

"I hope that you now can understand why it was less painful living in denial," he begged.

"You should've told me the truth, David. I was livin' a lie all this time!" I cried. "Why?" Hot tears began to roll down my cheeks.

"I'm sorry."

"How could you do this? You knew I grew up livin' in foster care and you saw how I was treated. Yet you sat on your ass and didn't decide to adopt me until I turned 12. What was the fuckin' point?" I demanded.

"After following up with your case, I contacted a caseworker in New York. She eventually gave us an update about your medical condition and the fainting episode that you experienced. One of the nurses told us about you possibly needing a matching blood donor if anything ever happened to you. It turned out that Brittney was the only match," David explained. "Sylvia and I talked about it and decided to take you in. She was a little resentful at first, but finally agreed, because that was a promise that I made to your mother many years ago," he said, sadly.

"You have to admit it, Cyndi. We did offer you love."

"No, you took me in because you had a guilty conscious," I said.

I didn't believe another word he said at this point.

"You're right Cyndi, I did," he admitted.

"Why didn't you want me when I was little? Didn't you ever think of me at times?" I asked, now feeling deserted.

"I've always thought about you, Cyndi. But Sylvia was never ready to accept you. Occasionally, I would bring it up, but she never wanted to talk about it. It wasn't until that day, when you first showed up at our house, that Sylvia had a change of heart."

"So, let me get this straight, you're sayin' that Sylvia had no problem with acceptin' Brittney from day one, but she couldn't accept me at all, right?" I asked, angrily.

"Yes."

"I really don't see what the fuckin' difference was here, only that Brittney wasn't as brown. Is that what it boiled down to?"

David couldn't answer. He sat with a remorseful expression that made me want to smack it completely off.

"I really wish I could go back and change things. Boy if I had the chance..."

"Forget it," I interrupted. "You did what you wanted to do. But tell me somethin' else, because I'm not fully understandin' this," I said sarcastically. "What was the difference with Sylvia only takin' in Brittney as her daughter as opposed to raisin' both of us together when we were younger? I mean, neither one of us are her kids for real?"

David began to fidget in his seat.

"You're not going to like this, but I have to tell you," David stated. "Sylvia was very resentful toward your mother once I confessed about our affair. She resented Shalana so much that she took her resentment out on you out of retaliation. So rather than leaving the children out of this mess, she chose to shut you out, simply to get even with Shalana."

"While she could forgive you and raise your daughter as her own?" I finished.

David began to cry.

"And you let her do it! You have no idea what I went through in those homes, do you?" I sneered.

"I can only imagine."

"Well, let me tell you. I was beaten whenever I wanted to go outside and play. I was burned on my arms and legs whenever I cried too much. I was starved and thrown in a hot- ass closet whenever I threw up their food that was rotten or not properly cooked. My foster parents would abandon me on the nights when they wanted to get drunk and high. They hated me," I said, remembering every horrid moment.

"I hope that one day you can forgive me."

"Let me ask you somethin', David. Does Brittney even know about our real mom?"

"No," he said, sobbing.

"Oh wow," I said, trying to register everything that was said. It was all coming at me so fast.

"Do you plan on tellin' her?" I asked.

"No," he admitted.

"I see. So, Brittney is gonna forever have all the finer things in life, while my ass suffers from those memories in foster care," I said.

"Cyndi, please, let's not discuss this anymore," he begged.

"Why? Are we gettin' uncomfortable here? Is the most respectful attorney finally takin' the hot seat?" I asked, sarcastically. "It's always about your precious reputation, right?"

"Please don't think of it that way," he pleaded.

I sat in silence, reeling with mixed emotions. I should have never been born.

"So then, you're not my father," I said as a final thought.

"No, I'm not," he said, tearfully.

"Then who is?"

"I really wish I could tell you that, Cyndi, but I don't have that information. All I know is that he was a Jamaican who was 12 years older than your mother."

David continued to wear his face of sorrow, which now had me feeling nauseous.

"What can I say, Cyndi? I was young and dumb. If I had the chance to go back and do it differently, I would. I swear it, Cyndi," he said.

"I have to go." As I stood up, I grabbed my bag and denim jacket and headed toward the front door.

"Cyndi, where are you going? You can't just leave like this," he asked, feeling desperate. "You don't even know where to go."

"Oh yes I do," I said defiantly.

"Here, take this," he pulled out wads of bills from his wallet. "That's the least I can do at this point."

"I don't want it! It's way too late to try buyin' love now," I said hatefully.

"Please take it," he begged.

"I'm not your daughter, David. So, back off. You didn't want me 17 years ago, so why feel bad now?" I opened the door and stepped out.

"Cyndi, wait!"

"Good bye," I said.

"I'm sorry!" he cried.

My mind was in a trance as I continued on my mission. I stared in front of me, thinking of where to go from here. Several cars whizzed by as, I walked along the highway in the night. Many people blared their horns angrily, trying to fight through the traffic, but I didn't care. I wanted to leave this forsaken place. I was tired of constantly being rejected. It was time that I started a new life.

Luckily, I had saved some cash from the last few paychecks from Cokey's, which allowed me to buy a ticket, once I reached the Greyhound terminal. I was scheduled to leave the next morning at 3:15am, which would get me to my destination a little before noon. I ended up sleeping on a hard row of chairs, using my bag as a pillow. My body was aching, but I didn't have any other choice. As the intercom announced the next departure, I woke up and saw that it was 2:45 a.m. I eagerly rose and headed toward the terminal for pre-boarding.

As I took my seat on the bus, I returned to sleep instantly. My 8 ½ hour nap was interrupted when the bus came to a halt in Mt. Laurel, New Jersey, which was about 35 minutes outside of Trenton. My final destination in Trenton unfortunately didn't have a bus terminal, which was why I had to go to Mt. Laurel. Realizing that I acted on impulsive, reality began to sink in and I became desperate. Where was I going to go from here? I didn't know a soul in this city and I wasn't able to afford a taxicab to ride to another destination. Shoving my hands into my jacket pockets, as I rose from my bus seat, I found my answer. I found a folded paper with Martina's address on it that I had hastily shoved in there when packing.

Immediately, I knew where I could go. Luckily, a middle-aged gentleman, who I met on the bus earlier, offered to help me. He had mentioned that he was also heading to Trenton once he arrived at the terminal.

As we emptied off of the bus, I saw the man meet an attractive young woman who I assumed was his wife. She resembled the model Eva Pigford, who was discovered on *America's Next Top Model*. Her skin was flawless and she was stunningly beautifully. At first, I assumed that she would be reluctant to help me since they didn't know me. But, the couple was nice enough to drop me off at a neighborhood near Martina's residence. I thanked them and walked off, hoping they weren't stalkers. I knew that I took a chance with my life with these people, but I didn't have a choice.

Martina answered the door, tired. It was obvious that she wasn't expecting any company. She unfastened the chains on the multi-locked door of her townhouse. She was dressed in a pair of grey sweats. Her hair was disheveled and her face was clean with no make-up. Never had I seen her without make-up, but it had been many years since I'd seen her at all. At first I wasn't sure what to say. I stood in front of her as we both appeared in shock. She stared at me until her expression brightened and she woke up.

"Cyndi?" she asked, in disbelief.

"Martina?"

"Oh my God! Cyndi!" she reached out and gave me a hug.

We embraced and cried in happiness. This was my one and only best friend. Marina would always be the sister that I could never have. We cried on each others' shoulders, thinking about painful memories that we endured together. Once we were calm, she let me inside her home. She had many questions to ask about me and I had plenty to tell her, since we had a lot of catching up to do.

"So, what are you doin' here? And how in the hell did you get here?" she asked excitedly. "Tell me what you've been doin' with yourself."

"It's a long story," I answered, walking into her kitchen. "I hope it's OK that I came. I know it was last minute, but I didn't have any other place to go."

"Nah, it's cool. Devon just left for work and I was about to go to sleep. I just got off work," she said. "And besides, you're my girl. You know you're always welcome at my crib."

"Thanks," I said, sipping hot tea. "Who's Devon?" I couldn't help but ask.

"I guess you can say he's my wonderful husband. Married life is cool, but we hardly see each other."

"Oh, sorry," I said.

"Girl, please. He's been gettin' on my nerves anyway. I'm sick of always comin' in trippin' over his empty video game cases or findin' his sneakers on the table," she complained, rolling her eyes. "Man that irks me!"

"Why did you marry him?" I asked.

"Honestly, it was the only way out. I got sick of hearin' my adopted parents rantin' and ravin' about how I needed to be saved. They drove me nuts with that crap. They used to make me sit with them and recite scriptures. It was crazy!" she said.

"Wow!"

"They were trippin' about how me and Devon were havin' premarital sex. They kept tellin' me that I had only two options, until I turned 18, which was to stop havin' sex or to get married and move out. So, I left."

"Damn!" I laughed.

"I kept tellin' them that I was on the pill, but it didn't matter. So, what's been up with you?"

I told her everything that happened, quickly recapping everything that occurred within the last five years. But I left out the details of Rashad. I didn't feel like bringing him up right now.

"Damn girl, you've been through some shit," she said sadly.

"I'm hungry as hell too. Can I have somethin' to eat?" I asked, realizing that my hunger pains had just started.

"Yeah, girl. What do you want?"

"I don't care," I said.

My body felt as though it had went without nourishment for a month. When she spooned the spicy bean and rice casserole with beef on my plate, I was ready to devour it. I scraped her plate, wishing that I could have seconds.

"Damn, girl!" she laughed.

Once I finished, she led me upstairs to the guest room.

"Well now that you're settled in, I'm gonna be in my room knocked out. Make yourself at home, and don't worry you can stay as long as you need to," she offered.

I thanked her and gave her another hug as I cried.

"It's cool. You know we go way back," she said.

During the last five years, I had never gotten this much hospitality from my own sister. But here I was at my friend's home and she offered all of what she had, when she barely had enough for herself.

"Well, it'll only be for a few days. No longer than a week," I said, thinking of my plan.

"That's cool," she hugged me again and headed toward her bedroom.

In a moment I was asleep and feeling completely cozy, until I woke up in the middle of the night. I didn't realize that I had slept the entire day. After heating up a box of macaroni and cheese, I explored Martina's home. She had a nice, furnished apartment.

She had beige carpeting throughout the entire apartment. Wicker furniture sat in the living room with pink and green plush pillows. A white ceiling fan spun at a slow speed from her sloped ceiling, which was adjoined to her kitchen. Her kitchen was designed in tan hues with a small table and matching table cloth. Her beige tile matched the curtains that covered her circular windows.

The kitchen chairs were soft with brown cushions. Upstairs, she had two bedrooms and a small bathroom. Inside her room, she had posters of various Rap artists. The dresser was tan with assorted decorations; a dark blue comforter was thrown on her queen-sized bed. Her guest room had a twin-size bed with a deep green comforter and matching fluffy pillows. The walls were plain and bare, but the room was still inviting. As I sat in front of the TV in the living room, I watched her *Dave Chapelle* DVDs and ate ice cream. A portrait of Martina and Devon sat on top of the TV.

They looked so happily in love, wearing matching blue and white sweatsuits. I assumed that Martina and Devon were visiting a park, since they were posed near a set of swings. His buffed arms wrapped around her, as they smiled.

I had to admit that Devon was attractive. He resembled Tyrese Gibson. His dark eyes had a sexy, penetrating glare and his lips looked sensuous. His hoodie covered his head, but I could tell that he was bald. Devon was completely covered in this picture, but I could tell that he maintained his physique quite well.

"You picked a good one, Martina," I said.

If only Rashad and I could've stayed in love! At this point, all I had were fond memories.

Chapter 14

The next day, I woke up early and had a quick breakfast. Martina and Devon were still asleep, as I walked out the front door. I caught a bus to an underground station and caught a train toward my destination. This was the day that I had waited for. I was ready to find information on my mother. Hopefully a staff member could tell me where she was so that I could meet my mother for the first time in 17years. As I entered the correctional facility, I became nervous and anxious. What would I say? Would she actually remember me? What if she didn't want to see me? I had so many thoughts in my head that I didn't realize the lady behind the glass asked a question.

"How can I help you?" she repeated.

"I'm here to visit someone," I answered nervously.

"Visitation hours will be endin' soon, but you still have some time," she said. "Please present a photo ID and head toward the security officer down the hall on the right."

I did what I was told and requested to see Shalana Taylor. As I approached the security officer, she appeared to be irritated. Perhaps she was burned out from her job.

"And what is your relation to her?"

"I'm her daughter," I answered.

"You know you have to schedule a week in advance to come durin' visitation hours, right?" she asked, rolling her eyes impatiently.

"You're kiddin', right?" I couldn't believe what I was hearing. I wasted money on a train ticket for nothing!

"Woman, do I look like I'm playin'? You need to call the main office right below us and ask when visitation hours are," the security officer explained.

"Look lady, I don't have time for this. I came a long way to get here. Can I at least meet with her for a few minutes?" I begged.

"No honey, it doesn't work that way," she said sarcastically. "Just go downstairs and get the contact number for visitation hours."

"Whatever!" I fired.

By this time, other people were beginning to stare but I didn't care. I began to cry in frustration. What else could go wrong? As I was about to walk away, an officer approached us.

"What seems to be the problem?" he asked.

"I was tryin' to visit my mom for the last few minutes of visitation hours, but this heffa got rude with me!" I snapped.

"Excuse me!" she demanded.

"Please, Janet, let me handle this," he offered.

He motioned for me to follow him, as we headed down the hall. Janet remained in the doorway, executing more fury.

"OK, what seems to be the trouble?" he asked, as we entered an office. He sat behind his desk.

"All I wanted to do was come here to visit my mother. I know that I didn't make an appointment, but I really came a long way just to see her. If you could help me, that would be great," I blurted.

"OK, what's your mother's name?" he asked, trying to calm me down.

"Her name is Shalana Taylor."

"OK, give me a minute," he said while searching his computer.

"What was her name again?"

I repeated her name, hoping that he was familiar with her.

"Oh," he said, suddenly sounding confused. "It appears that she's been released."

"What!"

"It says she was released three years ago," he informed.

"Well where is she?" I asked anxiously.

I was excited that she was released, but also upset that I was getting the run around. I couldn't afford to waste any more money on bus fares.

"According to our records, she was transferred to a treatment facility," the officer read.

"Treatment for what?" I asked confused.

"I'm afraid that I can't give you that information," he stated.

"Well, can you tell me where she is? What treatment facility did she go to?" I asked, determined to know her location.

"I'm sorry, but I'm not allowed to disclose any more information."

What the fuck was this man good for? Here I was thinking that I was taking five steps forward, when I was really taking 10 steps back. I sat in his office chair and began to tear up.

Perhaps it was the pregnancy hormones that made me extremely sensitive that day. Or maybe the officer began to feel remorseful, because as I cried, he offered a Kleenex and asked me several times to calm down. But I couldn't.

"You don't understand. My mother hasn't seen me since I was a new-born. I don't even know her!" I cried.

He sat at his desk and sighed, as though he were caught in a difficult situation. "OK, let me see what I can do," he finally said.

He turned to his monitor again and quickly read the information. "OK, get ready, it's a lot," he said.

"I'm ready," I said, wiping my tears.

"Your mother is now in Yonkers, New York. She's been in their program almost 3 ½ years by next month. We have here that she's eligible for termination within two years," he read.

I continued to listen, making sure that I remembered every detail.

"You didn't hear this from me, but their address is 1500 14th Avenue and I have their phone number, too. Just remember to bring a photo ID with you when you go."

I grabbed a pen and jotted down her address.

"You have a long trip ahead of you, so good luck," he advised.

After thanking him, I leaped from my seat and ran out. Once I had the information, I caught a cab to the nearest

Greyhound bus station and was on my way to my next mission. Luckily, I didn't have too far to go. I would arrive in White Plains, 10 miles outside of Yonkers by 6 that night. The four- hour trip seemed to drag on, however I stayed awake the entire time.

"Hello, how may I help you?" a security officer asked, as he stood at the sensors.

"I'm here to visit someone," I informed, now becoming irritated with these procedures.

"I need to see a photo ID."

"Here," I said, wanting to shove it in his face.

Because I didn't have a driver's license, since my adoptive parents never provided me with a car to drive, I had to use a state ID. At first, I assumed the security officer was going to give me trouble, but luckily, he accepted what I had.

"Please remove all jewelry," he instructed.

After being checked with security sensors, a short, heavy-set woman led me to a set of tables and chairs and advised me to wait for 10 minutes. Wow, this was it! I thought. Ten minutes and I would meet my mother for the first time!

The brief wait eventually grew to a half hour. Just when I was ready to leave, the woman returned with a tall, slim, dark-skinned woman with short, slicked back hair. She wore a light blue uniform with brown flip flops.

"Ms. Taylor," the heavy-set woman began. "It's really important that you cooperate today, because you have a visitor."

"A visitor? You must be out of your mind. Nobody comes to visit me. At least not since eight years ago!" my mother complained. "Anyway, I got work to do."

"It's your daughter," the lady said.

My mother continued to babble and complain of being interrupted, until she suddenly spotted my face. Her expression immediately shifted from anger and hostility to tears of pain.

"You have 20 minutes," the woman informed before leaving.

For a moment, I wasn't sure what to say or what to do. For many years, I had envisioned this day. But at this time, I couldn't speak. Anxiety and tension had built up for so long. Eventually I spoke up, but became angry.

"So, it's you? It's really you," I spat.

"Yeah, it's me. I'm your mother," she said, taking a seat.

"I don't think so! My mother would have never left me to the system. Do you realize that I grew up believin' that you were dead!" I cried.

"Oh no, that's where you have all the facts wrong," she said, sadly. "I never left you. I've always loved you. What happened was..."

"Save it!" I interrupted. "You didn't give a damn about me while you were layin' up under different dudes. I think all you ever cared about was hustlin' and makin' money!" I fired. I began to storm out of the room.

"Wait! Come back! We still have time to talk!" my mother called.

"I don't have nothin' else left to say to you!" I yelled.

"Cyndi, please come back!"

I continued to run. I didn't hear anything else. My mind became fuzzy. I had many mixed emotions at this time. I was angry. I was sad and resentful. As I ran down the hallway,

I ran toward the security guard to collect my ID and jewelry and was ready to head back to Martina's. By the time I arrived at Martina's apartment, after my 4 ½ hour ride, I realized that she had just left for work. Devon was asleep. It was after midnight. It hadn't been two whole days yet and I only saw her one time. At this point, I understood Martina's pain. She mentioned that she and Devon hardly saw each other, because of their different work schedules. For the rest of the night, I processed everything that occurred that day.

This was an extremely emotional experience. I still felt bitter and resentful. But eventually, my feelings began to change. As I went to bed, I dreamed of my mother. I dreamed of her trying to escape from prison while she was pregnant with me. In the dream, our bodies became switched and I became her. I was the one running like a runaway slave through the woods on a cold, dark, winter night.

I saw myself running, as a mob of wild dogs and police officers chased me. Clutching my full-term pregnant belly and running on my last breath of air, I tried to reach the highway. I was hoping to arrive to a nearby hospital. Just when I was about to flag down a beam of bright lights from a car, I was suddenly pulled back. I felt a pair of hands seize me by my shoulders, which ended my freedom and desperation for happiness.

I woke up in a pool of sweat crying, Nooo!"

I layed in bed and sobbed, feeling confused until I eventually understood my dream. My dream was the missing piece to the puzzle of my life. My mother was a fugitive while carrying me. Yet, she wanted so badly to escape, so that she could try to create a life for us. But unfortunately, cruel times had stolen that from us. I sat up in bed and finally came to a realization. My mother had to give me up for many reasons. If only she could forgive me now!

The next day I caught another bus to visit my mother again. I was on my last dollar, of the money that I had saved. But, I figured that money could be easily replaced. Yet, time spent with my mother could not. I realized that I never gave her a chance to tell her side of our story.

"So, you're back," she said.

"Yeah," I answered, feeling remorseful. "I know that I didn't give you a chance to tell your side yesterday, and that was wrong."

"What is it that you wanna know?" she asked. "I know that it's too late to make up for 17 years, but I sure as hell wanna try. Is there somethin' that you need?"

"I just wanna know the truth. I talked to David the other day, but now I wanna hear it from you," I answered.

"What did he tell you?"

I soon blurted the entire story of what David revealed, describing every detail of what he shared. I talked about my rough childhood in foster care and described the rocky transition of when I became adopted and met my half -sister. I even disclosed what occurred with Rashad and how he left me. As we talked, our dynamics began to change. I now didn't feel as though we had the ex-con/ visitor relationship anymore. We were now talking more like mother and daughter. We were bonding.

"Well, I must say," she said, smiling. "That sounds a lot like him. That's exactly what David would say, alright," she began to light a cigarette. "But all that doesn't surprise me," she snickered while taking a puff.

"What happened, Mom?" I asked, tears building up.

She sat back, took another puff on her cigarette, and took a deep breath as she crossed her arms and started to smile. "I was just a year older than you when I got into this mess," she said.

"My mother had just put me out of the house, because I gave her so much hell. She raised me the best way that she could in New York, but my mother had to show me tough love. I headed straight to New Jersey with little experience on the streets. I was very naïve, but I had to learn the hard way.

"Little did I know that a nightmare was waitin' for me around the corner. Times grew tough but I was determined to live on my own. Now that I was homeless, I had empty pockets with no income. The only type of work I could get was at fast food or convenient stores. But I wanted fast money. I was hungry for big fortunes.

"So, instead, I became a dancer. A club owner, who I knew, let me work for him. He knew that I was under 21, but as a token of payment, I did other work for him, if you know what I mean," my mother informed. "It was my way of thankin' him for keepin' it on the hush about my real age. But I was a good-ass dancer. It didn't take much for me to learn," my mother continued. "I learned really quick."

"There were times when I got hustled. I got robbed a couple times. I went without food sometimes. I've even been assaulted. But bein' in that line of work leads to that lifestyle. I slept in spots wherever I could lay my head, like sleazy motels, bus stations, and even pimp spots. But I couldn't go back. I was afraid of my mother rejectin' me. Instead, I continued to suffer on the streets.

"That night when I met David was like a princess meetin' her prince in a fairy-tale. After seein' my performance, he asked for a private dance and I gave him one. His boys cheered the whole time. Later on, he took me out for a few drinks and eventually, I ended up in his bed.

"From then on, he took care of me. David wined and dined me every night. He was the man I would fantasize about each time I laid with different dudes. Our relationship was perfect in my eyes, because he took me in and provided a home for me, makin' all sorts of promises. He took care of everything.

"I actually believed him. In my mind, I thought we had a lotta potential of settlin' down until he made his confession. David was married. With nowhere else to go and no one to turn to, I stayed with him. By this time, I had quit my job and money was gone again. But, I had the pipe dream of him leavin' his wife, since he swore up and down that he and his wife were hangin' on loose strands.

"Plus I was pregnant with your sister by then. So I didn't really have a choice, since I was startin' to show. David swore that he loved me and the day of his divorce were comin' closer. But instead, he was draggin' his feet with signin' the papers. Months passed and I delivered Brittney. Of course, I was heartbroken and depressed, still strugglin' to make ends meet. I now had to provide a home for your sister.

"I finally decided to look for a music career. I met your father at a club. Kaihri. That was his name. He was a handsome brotha. A tall, dark glass of water from Jamaica. I met him and instantly fell in love with his chocolate self. But, he was trouble. Your father worked for my ex- manager, as a bouncer. But he hustled on the side. Stars were definitely in my eyes, when I first met him.

"We went out a few times and he became fond of Brittney. I was ready to leave David for your father, because David was still playin' games with my head, tellin' me that he was gonna leave his wife, but I was tired of it.

"Within 10 months, I became pregnant with you. Kaihri had plans for me to start a singin' career. He wanted to form a Caribbean band similar to Square One and have me as the lead singer, like Allison Hinds. He talked up a storm about how I would travel and meet other celebrities. Kaihri also wanted to open a club in Jamaica. He had all sorts of business ideas. But he was runnin' from the law.

"As I carried you into my third trimester, I came home to David and announced that I was leavin'. It was over and I was fed up with him. At first he begged me to stay, cryin' and apologizin', until he suddenly became very mad. His agreement was to let me go, but he wanted to take Brittney.

"We fought and argued like cats and dogs until he pushed me and I fell. He was enraged that I had a second child with another man, especially a black man. That really upset him the most. But I didn't give up. I got up and ran after him. My body was sore, and I ran as fast as I could, but couldn't catch him.

"Cryin' hysterically, I ran inside the house and called your father, tellin' him what happened. Your father was upset. He wanted to practically kill David for nearly causin' me to miscarry. But he was ready to make things happen for us. Kaihri had planned, for many months, for us to leave. He already had our plane tickets. Everythin' was planned perfectly, except for one thing. Brittney was missin' and I wasn't leavin' until I had her. So we came up with a plan. Our plane was scheduled to take off that night and we knew where David lived. During that time David and his wife used to have a place in Jersey. But anyway, I was ready to scoop her up.

"Other people may call it kidnappin', but I don't see it that way. She was mine and I had every right to take her. Kaihri and I would have made it out, if things didn't become so fucked up. While David and his wife were throwin' a party, I walked right inside and snatched my baby up. Nobody blinked or stared twice at me since the doors and windows were wide open. Everyone was too busy gettin' high or drunk, or indulgin' in some crazy sex shit. But, I walked into their little nursery and left with my baby.

"Kaihri and I were so close until the cops busted us as we were about to get on the plane. We were charged with havin' stashes of marijuana in our bags, due to his partner settin' us up. Kaihri was charged with drug traffickin' and they charged me as an accomplice. They gave your father 20 to life, since he already had a felonious history. Then they slapped me with 14 at a women's prison. David and his wife got full custody of Brittney.

"His wife hated me. I think it was not only for sleepin' with her man, but also, because she couldn't have any kids. Your father and I kept in touch through letters with help from a friend on the outside. Our plan was to escape prison and flee to Jamaica, as we planned before. The last night I carried you, I ran through the woods.

"I was tryin' to run to your father where he was waitin' for me in a semi- truck along the highway. Kaihri had connections for gettin' that truck from another source on the outside. Unfortunately, I slipped on a bank of snow and fell, and that's when my water broke. You were ready to come into this crazy-ass world, but I wasn't ready for you to come.

"I struggled to get up, since I was in so much pain. The security guards found me, and grabbed me as Kaihri took off. I ended up havin' you in prison. After you were delivered, they took you from me and then I heard that you were placed in foster care. I tried, several times, askin' David to take you in; but he, many times, refused and wanted to keep Brittney only. I never saw or heard from your father again.

"Throughout the years, I tried to contact you in every way I could. I would ask my attorneys to locate you, so that I could send you letters. But they wouldn't help me. It wasn't easy. David always had the money and access to do whatever he wanted, but rather than helpin' me, he chose to live under the false pretense that I was dead. I suppose that was his way of shuttin' me out of his life for good."

When my mother finished her story, I sat in complete silence from shock. I wasn't sure what to say anymore.

"I kept up with you as much as I could. Please believe that. I knew that you weren't bein' treated right, but there was nothin' I could do," she said tearfully. "Why do you think you were shuffled around so many times?"

I couldn't answer. I continued to listen in shock.

"Once I was assigned a better attorney, he helped with trackin' you down," she said. "That's when I asked him to see that you be adopted. Of course, several years had passed, but I figured that it was either now or never. It took so long to get David and Sylvia to take you in. But they did it.

"I figured, that I at least, owed you that," she explained. Tears began to well up in her eyes.

"Mom!" I cried. It was a word that I thought would never become a part of my vocabulary.

"I'm so sorry," she apologized, now rising.

I stood up and stared at her as we cried. I wasn't sure what to do at this point. A handshake seemed impersonal, after we shared so much in the past hour. Somehow, I couldn't leave yet. Our visit wasn't over. All I could do was continue to cry, until she reached toward me.

I accepted her embrace and continued shedding tears, making up for those long years of separation. "I love you so much," she said.

Although I was close to adulthood with a child on the way, I couldn't help but cry like a baby. All my life, I lived a lie, believing that she was dead. Yet she was trapped inside the system, where she couldn't touch me. Many years I lived in confusion and had so many questions about myself. Yet, today I could finally put everything together. Once we became calm, we sat down and changed the subject.

"So, you're pregnant, huh?" she asked, trying to smile, as she wiped away her tears.

"Yeah," I sniffled.

"What are you gonna do?"

"I don't know," I said, now feeling lost.

"Well, whatever you decide to do, please promise me that you won't make the same mistakes I did," she pleaded. "If only I could turn back time. There's a lot of things I would have handled differently."

"Well, what's done is done," I said.

As I stared at my mother, I was able to see that she had once been a stunning beauty during her younger years. I even saw the resemblance that my sister and I shared with her. For many years, I constantly wondered whose features and personality I had. My mother was a slim, dark-skinned woman, now in her mid 30s. She had almond-shaped eyes with the same high cheek bones that Brittney and I had. My mother's hair was much shorter than mine with a thinner and straighter texture. Her nose was narrow and her lips were full, but not as full as mine. But now, my mother appeared older, due to the harsh times she'd endured. Her eyes that probably were once full of life, now looked tired.

"What did my father look like?" I asked.

As if she knew I soon would ask, she pulled out a small photo from her breast pocket and tossed it across the table toward me. "You got your father's height," she said.

There was my father, posed up against a tree with his broad, toned biceps folded across his buff chest. He wore a pair of black and white pin-striped pants with suspenders and a wife-beater underneath. I saw that he also sported a black hat that was cocked to the side. Once I saw his photo, I understood why my mother became so infatuated with him.

He had my Hershey complexion with dark, luring eyes that appeared mischievous. His nose was broad and his lips were similar to mine. "You got his smile, too," she said.

As I stared at him again, I saw that she was right. His smile was bright, which enhanced his photogenic appearance. His mustache gave him the look of the actor, Idris Elba who starred in the movie *Daddy's Little Girls*. After taking a good look at my father I was able to see similar characteristics that we shared. If only I could see him now.

"Where is he now?" I asked, hoping that I could one day meet him too.

"I don't know," she replied, teary-eyed.

The justice system had been extremely cruel and unfair to us. There would never be a time for my family to reunite!

When our visitation hour reached its end, I embraced her, promising that I'd visit again. After catching my final bus into town, I returned to Martina's. I walked inside and found her sitting on her couch facing her TV, that wasn't on. She appeared to be deep in thought.

"Hey!" I announced, walking in.

"What's goin' on?" she appeared concerned.

"Nothin' much," I answered.

"You've been here two days and we hardly saw you," she explained. "Are you in some kinda trouble? 'Cause I know you've been runnin' around here like a chicken with his head cut off. It's been really weird."

"No, I'm not in trouble," I answered, now almost finding her reaction humorous.

"Then, what's the deal?"

I took off my jacket and sat beside her, as I took a deep breath. So much had happened, where was I to begin? I finally told her every detail of how I discovered my mother's identity and fled from my adoptive home. I described the experience of meeting my mother for the first time, and the fact that I was three months pregnant. Martina listened intently, absorbing everything.

"Wow!" she shrieked, once I finished. "You've really been through some shit!"

"Yeah, no kiddin'," I complained.

"That's good that you got to meet your mom. At least now you know that she's alive," Martina said.

"I don't know what to do," I said.

"Oh my God! I can't believe you're pregnant!" she cried, hugging me. "Have you decided what you're gonna do yet?"

"I think so."

"OK, what?" she asked, eagerly.

"I think I wanna keep it."

"Really?" she asked.

"Yeah."

I began to stare at the floor. "I'm sorry I didn't tell you about it earlier. I didn't want you to think I was a 'ho," I said, now feeling ashamed.

"Girl, please, as much as I did in my past. You're an angel compared to the shit I've been through."

"What do you mean?" I asked.

Martina disclosed incidences of contracting STDs in her past. She talked about the times when she would wake up in strange places in her underwear, after going to different parties. As she continued disclosing her past, Martina began to talk about final memories of her mother. She mentioned how her mother was happy and vibrant until their entire family was taken out.

"There's not a day that goes by without me still havin' those crazy- ass dreams," she said, crying.

"Do you know who it was?" I asked, referring to their killer.

"No, but I'll never forget his face. Devon doesn't know it, but I sleep with a Glock beside my bed."

I hugged my best friend, allowing her to shed her tears of pain, until she remembered my situation again. "So, wait a minute," she said. "You're tellin' me that you're havin' this baby by yourself?"

"I gotta do what I gotta do," I said. "You know? I should leave, because I need to find a job and a place to stay," I began to rise.

"You mean, you have no place to go?"

"No," I answered, now feeling embarrassed.

Impulsiveness had clouded my judgment for the past two days. I never considered the consequences of leaving home. My concentration was geared toward finding my mother. Not only was I pregnant, without the father, but I was homeless and didn't have a penny to my name. I now had to think for two.

"Well damn, you can stay here until you get yourself situated. Mi casa, su casa," she offered. "I'm serious."

"Thanks. And trust me I don't plan on stayin' that long. Hopefully no more than two months," I said. "And once I get a job, I'll be outta here." I now became determined.

"You can stay here as long as you need to. Come on now, I have a little niece or nephew that I'm gonna spoil now," she said, smiling.

Once I became settled in, I helped her prepare dinner. She cooked a burrito meal large enough to feed a family of eight. Periodically I snacked on nachos and salsa dip, since my cravings were starting. As soon as we finished setting the table, Devon walked in from work.

He stood in the doorway dressed in his UPS uniform. His brown leather boots were covered with dried mud, and his dark blue hoodie covered his bald head. Devon appeared to be exhausted and dirty, but he still had a pleasant appearance. I couldn't help but stare in confusion. He seemed to hold a similar expression toward me.

"What's up?" he greeted Martina.

"Hey, poppy, come here," she said excitedly, approaching him.

I watched them greet each other as they kissed and embraced. He hugged Martina as though they hadn't seen each other in several months. "You smell good," he smiled, while burying his face in her neck.

Martina leaned into him until Devon suddenly remembered that I was in the room. "What's up?" he greeted me, now feeling awkward.

"Hey."

"This is my friend, Cyndi. She's gonna be stayin' with us for a while," Martina announced.

"Oh shit! You're Cyndi?" he said, excitedly.

"Yeah," I replied, now feeling awkward.

"I've heard so much about you. It's good to finally meet you!" he suddenly came to hug me.

I returned the affection, now realizing that I had a second place that I could call home. These people would be my family. Once we finished dinner, they went upstairs while I cleared the table and loaded the dishwasher. Later that night, I ate more nachos and salsa dip, watching DVDs of Steve Harvey's stand-up comedy shows.

Chapter 15

*T*hroughout the rest of my pregnancy, I lived with Martina and Devon. My intention was to stay no longer than two months, but finding housing was difficult, because of my situation. I was still under-age. My 18th birthday wasn't for another three months. So in the meantime, I didn't have a choice but to stay with my friends, since I didn't want to live in another group home. My transition was rough, since I relied largely on public assistance, but Martina and Devon helped in every way they could. By this time, I was serving tables at a restaurant while attending night classes at a community college.

All of us had different schedules, which also helped with maintaining each others' space. Devon still worked third shift at UPS and Martina worked nights at a warehouse. Luckily, since I had enough experience from working at Cokey's, the manager decided to hire me immediately. I used my tips to help pay for books while applying for grants. My initial plan was to attend Spelman, as I previously had told David and Sylvia. But since I missed the deadline for applying for their scholarship, I couldn't get in. I also couldn't apply for other scholarships at other universities, since I never met their criteria. I either had the wrong major or was the wrong type of minority. Sadly, my plans were altered, but I tried to focus on the positive outcomes of my situation. As my delivery date drew closer, I became nervous.

I wasn't financially ready to be a parent. The only insurance I had was Medicaid, and I hated the quality of care I got from their medical centers. Martina, at times, would help with buying baby necessities and swore that she would baby-sit for free. Occasionally, I felt uncomfortable with her offer, because I felt that she was doing too much. But she never cared. "You know this makes us family, right?" she would sometimes ask.

It was almost unreal to me. For years, I sobbed for never having a real family that truly wanted to accept me. The foster home in Brooklyn was brutal and my adoption with the Kramers was never a smooth transition. I had a half sister who hated me and an adoptive mother who was ashamed of me. Meanwhile, David lived in denial, pretending that everything was perfect while denying me any real affection or love. But now that I was living with Martina and Devon, I truly felt like I belonged to a family. I truly felt blessed. Still, being young and naïve, as I was, the night that I went into labor was a nightmare.

It was a late Friday night in February. My contractions began while I was in class. I tried to walk to the restroom, but I couldn't make it. My pains became worse and my pants were soaked from where my water had broken. Luckily, one of the students called 911 for me and shortly afterwards I was transported to the ER. Another student contacted Martina from my cell phone, as I was rolled inside the ambulance. They reached her just as she was leaving from work.

"I can't do this!" I cried hysterically.

"You're gonna make it, don't you worry", one of the para-medics consoled.

"It hurts!" I screamed. I clutched the sides of the stretcher, as sweat began to drip down the side of my face.

"Breath!" the nurse yelled as I was rolled into the hospital.

At this point, I was ready to slap anybody who was in my way. I also wished that I could have kicked Rashad in his face right now. Why couldn't he have been here? The doctors and nurses coached, ordering me to push as hard as I could.

"Come on Cyndi, you can do it!" they yelled.

Martina had arrived and stood at my side, coaching me as she held my hand.

"This doesn't look good," I heard my obstetrician say.

"What the hell is goin' on?" I cried.

"It looks as though your baby is breach. We're gonna try to turn him around, but I really need you to work with me, Cyndi. I know you can do this," he said.

I began to cry until one of the nurses helped to calm me. I used all the effort that I had. The doctor asked for the sur-gical scissors. But for some reason, the room became silent. What was happening? Was he dead? After experiencing a grueling nine hours of labor, I finally felt my child come out.

The room became quiet again. Surely I didn't have a still-born? In a moment, a nurse went to scoop the baby's mouth and we finally heard a shrill cry. "Well, I'd say she's ready now!" my doctor laughed.

"She?" I asked.

"Oh my God, Cyndi, you have a little girl!" Martina cried in happiness.

"We're going to need to run some tests since you've experienced a rough delivery, but once all the test results come back, I'm sure everything will be fine," the nurse smiled.

"I hope she'll be OK," I said, as I stared into my daughter's face for the first time.

Martina and I continued to stare at the infant, until more emotions flooded. "She's so beautiful," Martina whispered.

"She has Rashad's eyes," I said in tears. I rubbed a few strands of her hair, still amazed that I was now a mother.

As I cradled her, I saw that she let out a tiny yawn. Martina and I couldn't help but laugh.

"So what are you gonna call her?" Martina asked.

"Sabrina."

2006

Two years had passed since I delivered Sabrina. She was my motivation for living. Not only was she beautiful, but she was gifted. Sabrina learned to walk and talk very quickly, by the time she was nine months old. She was potty- trained by age 2 and was inquisitive to learn all she could about life by asking *why* questions or imitating others. There were many times when I saw Rashad through her and missed him. He was really missing a true blessing in her. Sabrina had most of his features. Her eyes resembled his; she had his caramel complexion and wavy hair texture. The only features my daughter and I shared were my high cheek bones, nose and lips. Now that I was 20, I had already completed a two-year program at a community college and transferred to the University of Phoenix in New Jersey.

I now lived in Princeton, New Jersey, in a small apartment, where my rent was based on income. As I worked part-time as a medical tech at a family medical care center in the mornings, Sabrina attended a childcare program with Title XX funding. At nights I attended classes, while Martina and Devon baby-sat Sabrina. By this time, I decided to major in Health Services Management. Not only did I feel fortunate to have a support system with my best friend, but I also started dating a gentleman, Dominique, from my job.

Dominique was a Venezuelan family physician who was 12 years older than me. He spoke English with a Spanish accent, and was always dressed well in designer suits. I loved his swagger, as he made his rounds in the facility and flashed his charming smile at the females. He was a man who had more maturity and sophistication because of his advanced life experience. Word among the staff was that he was married and divorced twice. Everyone said that he was known to be a womanizer, but I didn't care. I never cared if he flirted with others at the job, because I knew that I was his main selection after hours. Each time he called my name, his voice would trigger my deep infatuation. I sometimes got butterflies in my stomach when in his presence. Or at times, I would feel heady, as if on cloud nine, if I stared at him too long.

"So where are we meeting tonight, Ms. Cyndi?" he asked, as we met in the cafeteria at work.

"I was kinda thinkin' about a movie. Have you checked out that new flick The 40 year old Virgin? That shit looks funny as hell," I laughed.

"How about dinner instead?" he asked, pulling me toward him. "There's a perfect spot that I want to take you to."

"Alright," I said, now glowing like a school girl. Anything he said was like music to my ears, since I loved hearing him speak.

"I'll tell you what," he compromised, "I can grab something on the way home and then we can check out that movie. Sound good?"

"Yeah."

"Alright, we'll talk later. See ya," he kissed me on the cheek and hurried off, while trying to regain his professional swagger.

Every once in a while Dominique and I would exchange flirtatious expressions, if we crossed paths. He would sometimes wink or flash his smile, which drove me crazy. Once my shift ended, I rushed to Sabrina's daycare to pick her up, and dropped her off at Martina's. Afterwards, I caught the bus to attend my night class at the Phoenix campus.

Unfortunately, I wasn't able to afford a car, but worked overtime, whenever I had the chance. My life was chaotic, but I didn't have a choice. Providing for Sabrina motivated me to pursue my ultimate goal even harder. Once I returned home from class, Dominique showed up for our date. Instead, we took off to a seafood place called *Crab Legs*.

"So, tell me more about yourself, Cyndi," he said once we sat at our table.

Dominique and I worked together for a year, but just started dating each other about two weeks before. Because of our work schedules and professional relationship, we never talked about our personal lives until now.

"Well," I started, while sampling clams, "I have a daughter. She's two, and she's extremely smart."

"And her father? Does she see much of him?" Dominique asked, chewing on his lobster.

"No, he's been out of the picture from day one."

"That's too bad," Dominique empathized.

"Hey, we do what we gotta do. But we'll be fine," I answered, trying to mask my pain.

"What's your daughter's name?"

"Sabrina Cheyenne Stone" I answered, proudly.

"That's beautiful," he smiled.

"Thank you," I said. "Now what about you?" I now wanted to avoid being put on the spot.

"Oh, well, as you probably already heard, I'm divorced. I have two kids, but they stay with their mother," he stated.

"I'm sorry it didn't work out," I said, now nibbling my shrimp.

"What was that you just said? Oh yeah, we do what we gotta do," he imitated humorously.

"How old are your children?"

"My daughter, Charisse, is 10 and Shamar is 8. They now live in Puerto Rico with their mother and grandmother. But I have visitation twice a year."

"I see," I said inquisitively.

"I heard that you got married twice, right?" I asked, trying to keep up with his status. "What happened with your second wife, if I may ask?"

Word about this guy swarmed faster than bees searching for honey, but I was determined to get the real scoop before I laid down with this man. I certainly didn't want to wake up and find a woman standing over my head with a skillet ready to strike!

"Yes, that's true," he answered. "My second wife miscarried with our child when she was four months pregnant. We went through so much; we finally decided to go our separate ways."

"Oh wow!" I gasped, suddenly feeling as though I probed too much.

"Hey, shit happens. I'll always love my ex-wife and do whatever I can to help her. But like I said before, we needed to heal."

"Here, let me help you with that," he offered flirtatiously.

I let him taste my fingers that were covered in butter sauce. He stared into my eyes, already mentally seducing me. I let him sample my finger tips, imagining his L.L. Cool J. lips caressing mine. Toward the end of our date, Dominique drove me to pick up Sabrina and then to our home. Since Sabrina was asleep, as I carried her inside, Dominique and I began to whisper.

"She looks a lot like you," he whispered.

"I get that a lot, but I can't see it. To me she looks a lot like her father."

"I had a good time with you Cyndi. I want to do this again. Maybe next time we could take Sabrina with us," he suggested.

"We'd like that," I answered.

Chapter 16

$\mathcal{F}$or the next three weeks, my attraction toward Dominique became stronger. He came to our home more often and started to spend more time with us. I couldn't ask for a better potential step-father. Dominique even helped by buying groceries for us. He spoiled Sabrina with toys, sweets and expensive clothes, and became my transportation. In the mornings we drove to work together, and some nights, he baby-sat Sabrina.

"You really do a lot for us, Dominique," I said one day.

"Some body's gotta take care of my two ladies," he said, smiling.

At times Martina mentioned that she hardly heard from us. "While you're up in your crib playin' wifey, you could give us a shout sometimes," she said humorously.

"My bad. I've just been busy," I answered, thinking about my priorities.

"That nigga must be puttin' in some good- ass work, 'cause we don't see you at all now," she laughed. "Is it that good?"

I couldn't help but laugh at her remark, but then I began to wonder. What if she was right? Was I spending too much time with him?

It was a Saturday afternoon when Martina called me from her cell phone. Since I didn't work weekends, I stayed home and worked on a research paper. Sabrina was down for a nap, as I sat in front of my TV set with scattered papers. Dominique was paged from his job, so he had to leave suddenly. I felt boggled down, while trying to cite different sources for my paper, but was relieved when I received her call.

"What's up?" she asked eagerly.

"Tryin' to get this paper outta the way that's due next week. This shit is no joke. We gotta have 15 sources in our paper with a word count of 2,500. I need a break," I complained.

"Cool, get dressed, 'cause I'm comin' to scoop you up."

"What?" I asked, surprised.

Before I could comment, she hung up. Within 20 minutes, Martina was at my door. She stared at my pajamas, disappointed, as I let her in.

"I know you ain't about to go sportin' them," she said, sarcastically. "Come on girl, we're goin' shoppin'!"

"I can't, I don't have a babysitter. And I just put her down."

"Well, bring her to my crib. Devon can watch her. He ain't doin' nothin' but playin' those stupid video games anyway," Martina said, rolling her eyes.

"Damn, I wanna go, but I can't," I moaned.

"Girl, come on. This is your only chance we get to hang out. And you just said that you needed a break," she begged. "I promise I won't have you out that long."

After a few attempts of convincing, I finally relented. "Alright, let me go change." I started up the stairs.

Martina and I spent the entire day together shopping. It felt good to be out since I was always cramped inside studying. "We should do this more often," I said, snacking on ice cream.

We had just finished splurging, when we decided to eat at the food court in the mall. "Hell yeah, I hardly get to see you," she said, eating a soft pretzel.

"You wanna hear somethin' crazy?" she asked.

"What?"

"I always thought I would become pregnant first. But look how things turned out." Martina said.

"And that's funny that you say that, because I always said that I would never get pregnant," I laughed.

I never, once in my life, imagined myself being in a committed relationship or settling down, raising kids. While I was growing up, boys never asked me on dates, until my sophomore year. I always felt that I blossomed too late.

"Me and Devon talk about it sometimes. He says he wants to have a boy, so that he can name our son after his brother," Martina explained.

"Well, whenever you two have kids, promise me that you won't be a fuck up like me," I begged.

"What?"

"I'm serious. I really fucked up. Don't get me wrong, I love Sabrina more than anythin', but I was really wantin' to be livin' in ATL makin' some Gs by now. No chance in that ever happenin' now," I said glumly.

"Don't say that, Cyndi, you got a lot goin' for yourself. You got a job, you go to school, and now you got a man who makes over 100 Gs. The man's got mad paper! What more could you ask for?"

"Yeah, you're right. But still, just promise me that you'll be smarter than I was," I suggested.

"Alright, shit!" she said, impatiently. "Now come on, there's two dudes over there that keep checkin' us. Let's see what they're about," she said excitedly. She grabbed my hand and we headed off toward their direction.

My advice obviously went in one ear and out the other, but I followed her to a table where two gentlemen sat. At first we tried to walk past them, pretending not to be obvious, but we were truly scoping them. One of them was a fair-skinned guy dressed in shorts and a T-shirt. The other was a dark-skinned dude, who sported jeans and a button-down dress shirt. Both were clean- cut and appeared intellectual.

"What's up?" the lighter one greeted.

Martina quickly spun around as though she were truly caught off guard, as they spoke to us. "Oh, hi," she said seductively.

"Are you two from around here?" he asked while eating some Chinese cuisine.

"Yeah," she answered.

I let Martina do all the talking, since she was enjoying playing the flirtatious role. She had a husband at home who truly worked hard and loved her dearly. But for some reason, Martina was starving for more attention.

As we talked, we learned that the gentlemen, named Tre and Malique, were students from the University of Phoenix. I eventually discovered that one of them was in a few of my medical classes.

"Well, you have to show us what Jersey's all about. We're from Baltimore," Malique, the darker one, suggested.

"You sure y'all ready for this?" Martina teased, enjoying their attention.

"There's gonna be an off the chain party with 50 Cent, G-Unit and Lil' Wayne performing tonight at the Red Lounge Club. You should check it out," Tre invited.

"Alright then," Martina agreed.

After exchanging phone numbers on our cell phones, Martina and I walked off. "Damn, they were fine!" Martina expressed, once we headed to the car.

"I don't think I'll be goin'," I said, trying to be responsible. "I have to stay home and look after Sabrina."

"Oh, come on," Martina urged. "Sabrina will be OK."

Why not? I thought. It's not like I get to do this very often. What can one night hurt?

It took me several months to lose the weight that I gained during my pregnancy. So, today I didn't have a problem fitting into my new outfit that I just bought. It was a leopard -print - fitted dress with spaghetti straps that accentuated all of my voluptuous places. Martina sported black, flare-legged pants with a sheer top that nearly showed all of her Victoria's Secret bra. Both of us wore black strapped sandals. She wore her hair down and I wore mine twisted up. By this time, my hair was past my shoulders, but I wanted to appear classy and sexy tonight.

"We look hot!" she cried.

"Yeah, we got it goin' on," I laughed.

That night I had the time of my life, experiencing the single life again. For some reason, all responsibilities were briefly pushed aside. Martina and I met with Tre and Malique and danced to all of 50 Cent and Lil' Wayne's hits. We tasted many drinks and shared several blunts, which led to more provocativeness.

After having her third drink, Martina was on the stage with the performers. She gyrated against 50 Cent, which caused more excitement from the men in the audience. As the rappers performed, Martina began to dance for the crowd, resembling similar moves as those depicted in the *Player's Club*. Toward the end of the performance, Tre and Malique wanted us to come home with them.

Martina was ready to hop in the car with them instantly, forgetting that she was married. What stopped us, was when Tre became sick from drinking too much. He started to heave, eventually throwing up. I finally returned to logical reasoning, not wanting to cheat on Dominique.

"Oh shit! Don't tell me that dude started hurlin'! He's definitely not gettin' any ass now!" Martina complained in her drunkenness.

"Martina, chill out. You got a husband at home who looks and smells a whole lot better than him anyway. Let's just go!" I fired.

"I'll take you home," Malique offered. "Let's get them in the car first."

I helped Martina, as Malique helped his friend. Martina was so drunk that she sat in the backseat and slumped against the window. Once I helped her get settled into her apartment with Devon and Malique's help, I decided to leave Sabrina upstairs. It was late and I didn't want to disrupt her sleep. I knew that if I tried picking her up, it would be difficult putting her back to bed at our house.

"Get home safe," Devon said.

"I will. See ya!"

As Malique dropped me off, he tried to offer a kiss, as he opened the car to let me out. As much as I didn't want to, since he was so polite, I had to stop him. "I have a boyfriend," I stated as his lips barely grazed mine.

"It's cool," he said politely. I had a good time. Maybe I'll see you around." He got into his car as I retreated up the stairs to my apartment.

I had only been dating Dominique for a few months, but I didn't want to jeopardize what we'd started. I truly liked him and wanted to keep him.

"Where the hell have you been?" a voice demanded before I had the chance to turn on the light.

"I stood in the darkness, startled. "Dominique?"

"Yeah, who else were you expecting? Maybe another boyfriend?" he asked rudely.

"You scared me to death. What are you still doin' up?" I asked, now turning on the light.

"Why are you still out?" he demanded.

"I went out."

"With who?" he asked.

"My friend."

"Who?" he yelled.

"Martina. Why you trippin'?" I asked, now feeling interrogated.

"Why am I trippin'?" he asked humorously. "Well, it's four in the morning and you're just walking in the door dressed like that? Plus, I saw you with your little boyfriend out there," he said enviously, now rising from his seat in the living room.

"Now, I'll ask you again. Where have you been?" he repeated as he came toward me on the stairway.

"Oh my God, that dude is not my boyfriend. He's just somebody who gave me a ride home," I defended sarcastically.

"Whatever. Where did you and Martina go?"

"We just went to the club. What's wrong with you?" I asked impatiently.

This was a side of Dominique I'd never seen before. He was beginning to annoy me now. Maybe I was better off getting with Malique.

"You could've called or texted me. I sat here waiting for you all night and Sabrina was up screaming, because you weren't here," he sneered.

"She's here?" I asked, now confused. I thought she was still at Martina and Devon's.

"Yeah, she's here. But that shows how much you really care. You wanted to go out with your friend. Or maybe your boyfriend," he accused.

"I just told you he's not my boyfriend!" I yelled.

What was it going to take to convince this guy that I was telling the truth?

"You fucked him didn't you?"

"You know what? I'm goin' to bed," I said, ready to head up the stairs.

He grabbed my arm, indicating that our conversation wasn't over. "Answer the question," he ordered.

"Let go of me."

"You're dressed like some kinda hoochie and you're telling me to let it go? I don't think so. Answer the question, Cyndi," he demanded.

"No, I didn't fuck him Dominique. Now let go of my arm," I said.

"I don't believe you. Take that shit off," he said.

"Dominique, I don't appreciate you talkin' to me like this. You need to leave," I insisted.

"I'll leave when I'm fucking ready," he said.

Now that we both were upset, I tried to calm the situation. Maybe I needed to explain why I was out, since he was only seeing it from his perspective.

"Dominique, you weren't here and I was bored. I haven't had the chance to see my friend in forever and we just wanted to hang out," I explained.

"Well, while you were out doing whatever, I was able to leave work early tonight and tried to plan a perfect dinner for us. But your ass wasn't here!" he fired.

"My bad. If I knew you were gettin' off early, I would've stayed home," I said.

"Well, like I said, you could've called or texted me. Sabrina was up all night screaming," he repeated.

"I'm sorry," I apologized, now feeling exhausted.

"Wait a minute," he suddenly began to sniff around my hair. "You've been smoking haven't you?"

"Yeah, so what," I answered, sighing.

"And you're trying to tell me that you didn't fuck? Bullshit, I know your ass was out there fucking," he accused. "Take that shit off. Take it off!"

"Dominique, you're trippin'!" I screamed tears now filling my eyes.

"You're out at some club doing God knows what, while leaving your child with strange men? That shit ain't cool. She needs to stay here with us," Dominique ordered.

"What the hell are you talkin' about? Devon is not a *strange* man!" I cried. "I've known him long before I've met you! You know that Martina and Devon are considered family."

"Bullshit, I know about that dude. He got in trouble for stealing cars one time," Dominique scoffed.

"That shit was done five years ago, when he got in trouble with his brother, but that has nothin' to do with this. Why you actin' like this?" I asked.

Martina once told me about a time when Devon was picked up for being in the wrong place at the wrong time. Devon had gotten involved in a fight at a club. His brother picked him up and attempted to drive him home. As they drove, the police pulled them over for reckless driving. While the police began checking the license plate, Devon's brother suddenly sped off, which lead to a chase.

Eventually, they were caught and prosecuted, since the car was stolen. His brother was incarcerated for five years. But Devon was released on bail after three days, since he truly didn't participate in the car theft. Unfortunately, he had to struggle with getting his record expunged, which left him a stigma on his reputation.

"Well, Sabrina won't be going over there anymore, since I don't feel comfortable with having her around an ex felon. And neither will you," he said.

"Dominique, you are really trippin'," I said, angrily.

"I said to take that shit off," he yelled, now ripping my brand new dress.

"Hey, I just bought this!" I cried.

"Shut up! You won't be needing it now!" he ordered.

"Get off of me!" I was in tears.

"Take it off or I'll take it off for you!" he fired.

Dominique continued to rip at my clothing and I tried to pull away and fight him off. But it did no good. Eventually, my dress was ripped in shreds, which left me completely naked in front of him. He even ripped my bra.

"Get up stairs and wash that shit off your face," he said disgustedly. He was referring to my make-up.

I ran upstairs into the bathroom and slammed the door.

"Don't come out until it's all off," he said from the hallway.

Once I finished washing my face, I wrapped myself in a bathrobe and sat on the floor, sobbing. Why did he have to act like this?

He tried to open the door but realized that it was locked. "Fine, you can stay your ass in there all night. I don't care. I don't need to make a whore into a housewife," he stated before walking off.

When he left, I checked on Sabrina, who luckily was still asleep. Then I went to bed, wondering what I did wrong. Dominique was gone early the next morning.

Chapter 17

*L*ater that morning, I called Martina and told her what happened. Although she was experiencing a severe hang-over, Martina still made an effort to listen to me.

"I don't care what you say, Cyndi, that dude is straight up crazy," Martina said. "I wish Devon would try to pull that shit on me. I'd knock his ass out!" she said sarcastically.

I sat on the other end trying to justify his behavior. "I don't know, Martina; he said he was up all night waitin' for me. Maybe he tripped, because he was worried."

"Whatever!" Martina shrieked.

"I don't know what to do," I said.

"You need to leave that dude alone," Martina advised. "I gotta give it to you, he's cute and I'm sure that the sex is off the chain, but you can get with other doctors who would treat you way better."

"That's easier said than done, Martina," I said, sadly.

"I'm sure it is. But you gotta do what you gotta do. Put that nigga out and move on. Get the locks changed now that he's got a key to your spot," she added.

"Yeah, maybe," I said, feeling discouraged.

"Try gettin' with a dude who doesn't show schizophrenic tendencies this time. Maybe that Malique dude. He was feelin' you."

"Yeah, true," I said.

I wanted to take her advice, but somehow, I had a feeling that I had a mess on my hands that wouldn't be easy cleaning up.

"Just think about it," she offered.

We sat on the phone talking until she, all of a sudden, became sick again. "Oh shit, I gotta go!" she yelled.

Before she slammed the phone down, I heard her begin to throw up.

"Bye Martina," I said, now becoming disgusted after hearing her heaving sounds.

Sabrina began to sense that I was sad, as I sat on the couch in front of the TV. She stared up at me from her building blocks and asked, "Mommy, why you cry?"

"I'm not cryin', Sabrina," I lied, quickly wiping my tears. "I'm just really tired."

"Oh," she answered, confused. I watched her pick up one of her dolls and begin to cradle it. "Mommy's not crying. She's just tired," she imitated to the doll.

I continued to sit on the couch, wishing that I could live in a make-believe world with her. Perhaps it would be a better place.

Dominique returned later that evening with a bouquet of roses for me and a teddy bear for Sabrina, which she adored immediately.

"It's my bear now!" she proudly announced, while hugging it.

He came into the kitchen and embraced me. "I'm sorry, baby."

"You really hurt me. You said some off the wall shit to me last night and I don't appreciate how you were treatin' me," I said, upset.

"I know it. I'm sorry. I don't know why I was trippin'. Maybe it's because I saw you with that dude," he explained. "I saw how you were dressed and I flipped out. Guys get different ideas when they see women in those type of clothes."

I wanted to assure Dominique that he had no reason to worry. All I wanted was him. No other man could ever take his place, since I loved him.

"But Dominique, you don't have to worry. I..."

I was quickly silenced with a kiss. I leaned into him and returned the affection, tears blurring my vision.

"It won't happen again. I promise," he swore, kissing me again.

Later, we put Sabrina down for a nap and went to engage in make-up sex. Our ecstasy lasted into the late hours of night time. When Sabrina woke up complaining that she was hungry, I fed her a plate of chicken Mc Nuggets and lemonade. Once I put her back to bed, I joined Dominique, where we finished our exotic activity until the early morning.

Dominique kissed my inner thighs, traveling up to my womanhood, making me tremble. He took his time and I enjoyed every minute of him tasting my sweetness. As he came up to my face, he gently kissed my hair and pushed himself inside me. Condoms were no longer an option at this point, since we had discussed having a monogamous relationship.

"You don't ever have to worry about me walking away from my responsibilities," he said to me one day.

My first reaction was to not trust him, since Rashad had made a similar comment. But not too long after, I was prescribed the Nuva Ring. So after that, I didn't feel as vulnerable and anxious.

"I love you, Dominique," I said, clinging onto him. I didn't want this moment to end. His love could be so beautiful, when he wasn't upset.

"I love you too, baby. Promise me that you'll never leave me. Promise me," he urged, while penetrating me.

"I promise."

Six months later, my lease ended and we moved into a three-level home. Our new home was located in a community full of physicians and attorneys, which was a different world for me. I wasn't used to living inside a highly affluent neighborhood, since it was even more prestigious than David and Sylvia's community. Inside our home, we had three bathrooms and four bedrooms. One of them was made into an office and a playroom for Sabrina. The remaining rooms, we used as guest rooms, with hopes of making one of them into a bedroom for a second child. Our kitchen was designed elaborately in beige and white.

We had an island with bar-stools in the middle. A glass table with beige, soft-cushioned chairs sat in front of large doors that led to our huge backyard. A few weeks later, Dominique purchased a swing set and playhouse for our yard. We had a two-car garage for his car and the brand new Lexus that he bought for me. We used our lower level as an entertainment space.

We had a large-screen TV with a sofa set down there. Our couches and ottoman were black with large, white plush pillows. We had several CDs of different genres and so many DVDS that we could have stocked at a video store. I loved our home, because I finally felt that I had the perfect set-up that I always wanted for my family.

"I like it Mommy!" Sabrina cried excitedly as she ran into her new bedroom. She had every Bratz and Barbie doll collection, as well as tons of new games and clothes.

"I love it here too" I laughed, picking her up.

"I just want to see you happy," Dominique said.

As I stared at him, I saw that he was smiling, but his eyes were teary. I quickly became concerned. Surely he didn't believe that he needed to buy our love? I thought.

Ever since his last tantrum, Dominique periodically experienced mood swings. There were times when he smiled and he had lots of love to give. At other times, he became angry and aggressive. During the good times, I tried to make the best of them, but it seemed my efforts were never good enough. Moving in together was supposed to make us closer. Instead, it seemed we were drifting further apart. Our problems became worse. Dominique became more controlling and possessive.

He even became violent. As much as I loved our home, Sabrina and I stayed with Martina and Devon many nights, because Dominique's anger was so bad. Sometimes I would send Sabrina to stay with them while I stayed at home, so that Dominique and I could resolve our issues. He always swore that I was sleeping around. He always seemed para-noid and insecure. We once argued about it.

It was a late Thursday night when I returned home from night class. Once again, he was home early and had waited awhile for me to return. This was on a night I had met with my classmates about a group project we had to complete. Unfortunately, my reason for being late getting home wasn't believable to Dominique. He yelled and made threats of throwing me and Sabrina out on the streets, then he struck me. I wanted to leave him. No matter how many times I made attempts to leave or file charges, Dominique begged me to return home.

He would blow up my phone leaving multiple messages, begging in tears, for me to return. "I know I fucked up, Cyndi," he would say. "But please come home and give me another chance. I promise I'll be a better father for Sabrina this time."

Because of guilt and pity, I would relent and believe his story. As we made up, he would try pampering me with gifts or bandage our emotional wounds with sex. Previously, I enjoyed our passion, because I honestly believed that he wanted to make our relationship work. But over time, I felt used, because I knew that we would just go down the same road again.

"I can't do this anymore, Dominique," I said, packing a bag. "It's over! We're done!"

"What?" he seized me and pressed me into a wall. "You swore that you would never leave me. Do you remember that?" he reminded.

"You need to get off me Dominique. Get off!" I screamed. I shoved him.

His grip became tighter and he shoved me harder into the wall, which stung my shoulder blades. I felt it radiate down my lower back.

"Don't you ever shove me like that again, you got that? And you're not leaving me! You don't leave until I tell you to leave, bitch!" he fired, slapping the side of my head.

I called Martina and asked her to pick up Sabrina. I wanted to leave, too, but I couldn't, because I was afraid. He locked me inside our bedroom, threatening that I better not think about sneaking out. As she collected Sabrina, Martina called the police. Within 15 minutes, they rushed to the front door and took him in. An officer broke down our bedroom door to let me out and I gave a statement. Once we finished, I drove to Martina's. But this process wasn't easy either.

Since Dominique had the money to afford a powerful attorney, he was able to get off. The police sent him home after paying a large bail. Rather than going through the embarrassment in our neighborhood of publicly splitting up, Dominique decided to attend counseling and anger management.

"I promise I'll get all the help that I need, baby. Just please don't leave me. Don't throw away what we have. I don't know what I'd do without you," he cried.

He swore that our battles would come to an end, but a month later, we had another argument. By this time, I practically walked on egg shells. I tried to be cautious of not saying something wrong, wearing the wrong outfit, or cooking something that he wouldn't like. I even tried rushing home, so that I wouldn't be late from work or night class. But no matter what I did, I could never please him. I now lived in paranoia.

"Cyndi, you gotta leave him. What the hell are you waitin' on?" Martina asked as we drove along the highway during a road trip.

Sabrina was lying across the backseat in the SUV that we rented. We had planned a road trip to Virginia Beach simply so I could get away from Dominique. Martina requested a weekend off from her job, and my university was on spring break. So, I had free time on my hands.

"I hear what you're sayin', Martina. You're right. Dominique isn't perfect, but I have to admit that he does take good care of us," I said. "I'd be stupid to walk away from what we have."

"Is all that really worth it, though? I mean, he makes plenty of paper and you got a spot that could house a celebrity, but what if somethin' happens to you? Do you wanna go outta here as a rich battered wife?" she asked.

"What other choice do I have? I can't afford to move out," I stated sadly.

Dominique had access to everything that I couldn't afford. He was now paying for Sabrina's enrollment at a new, fancier childcare facility, and he handled her medical bills through his health insurance. There would be pros and cons to consider before I left Dominique.

"You know you always got a spot with me and Devon."

"Thanks," I said, tearing up.

"Girl, don't worry about it, you know we family."

I sat and thought about my situation with Dominique. Why did this have to happen? When times were good, we had the best chemistry. The other day, we had dinner at an elaborate restaurant and then took Sabrina to an arcade. Then we left Sabrina with a baby-sitter and spent a weekend at a resort in New England. He was so gentle and genuine there. I truly loved him when he behaved that way.

As we spent time together, we talked about our future plans. Dominique mentioned that if I stayed with him another three years, that Sabrina could be enrolled at a private school with all expenses paid. Despite that he could be cruel to me at times he was a good father to Sabrina. He had all her needs taken care of. Who else would give Sabrina this fatherly love and support? Certainly not Rashad!

"Mommy, I gotta go pee," Sabrina whined, now waking up as she interrupted my thoughts.

"Hold on, lil' mama. We're almost there," Martina smiled through her rearview.

I began to snicker. Sabrina's concerns were always perfectly timed whenever I was upset or concerned. Because, whenever she experienced a toddler crisis, I found it comical. Once we reached Virginia Beach, Martina checked us into a Holiday Inn, as I took Sabrina to the restroom. I hadn't realized how fast my daughter was growing up, until I saw her use the adult toilet by herself.

Normally, she needed assistance, if she wasn't using her trainer seat. But today, she didn't need my help. I was so proud of her, already transitioning from her pull-ups. "Look at me, Mommy," she bragged, smiling.

"Alright, you go girl," I cheered.

Cyndi

I began to glance around, wondering if others were present to hear our embarrassing moment. Luckily, the restroom was empty and I was glad. If only Rashad could share some of our moments. Once we got settled in, we decided to visit the beach.

Chapter 18

"Alright, let's go," Martina announced.

"I wanna swim. Swim, mommy?" Sabrina begged.

"Well, you heard what the little lady said. Let's go swimmin'!" Martina agreed.

"Alright then," I said with a laugh. "Sometimes I wonder which one of you is the spoiled brat."

That Friday afternoon, we took Sabrina to the beach and tried, to teach her to swim. Martina collected seashells and showed Sabrina different fish as I socialized with lifeguards. Escaping from Dominique was the best vacation I ever had. I felt so free and relaxed. The next day, we took Sabrina to see *Lion King 1 ½* at the movies and went to the park.

That whole weekend was fun until Sunday afternoon. Martina and I were packed and ready to return home. I was dreading seeing Dominique again with his unpredictable moods and temper. Before we headed for the highway, Martina made a stop at a convenience store.

"Who wants ice cream?" she announced.

Me!" Sabrina cheered.

"She doesn't need any, Martina. She's already bouncin' all over the walls from all that candy she ate," I warned.

"Aww," Martina moaned in disappointment. "Well, can she have just one scoop?" she begged.

When I didn't answer, Martina continued trying to convince me. "What flavor do you want?" she asked.

"Strawberry," I answered, rolling my eyes. "You know you turnin' my daughter into a brat, right?"

"All girls are supposed to be brats, what are you talkin' about?" Martina asked humorously.

As she pumped the gas, I took Sabrina inside to use the restroom and buy the ice cream. As I turned my back to use the ice cream machine, Sabrina suddenly disappeared.

"Sabrina!" I called frantically.

I ran around the store calling her name but couldn't find her. "Sabrina! Sabrina!" I dropped the cups of ice cream onto the floor, desperately looking for my daughter, until I finally found her near an area of toys.

"What's wrong with you?" I scolded. "Don't you ever run off like that again. Do you hear me?"

Sabrina stared at the floor and pouted.

"Now get over here and stay where I can see you!" I demanded. I grabbed her tiny hand and headed toward the ice cream machine to make us another swirl.

Apparently my lecture wasn't strong enough, because as I stood in line to pay for the desserts, Sabrina began to run around the store while screaming at the top of her lungs.

"Get over here!" I yelled.

Sabrina ignored me.

"Your daughter is quite feisty, isn't she?" the cashier chuckled.

"She won't be so feisty when she gets home," I said. "Sabrina, what did I tell you about talkin' to strangers? Get over here!"

"Mommy, look!" Sabrina, called excitedly. "A doggy! Look at the doggy!"

Before I could stop her, she ran toward the giant Collie and began to pet him. The dog barked loudly and wagged his tail.

"Sabrina, stop!" I yelled, now stepping out of line to get her.

She was gonna get it for sure!

"It's OK, she's not botherin' me. I think Ginger likes her," a voice informed, laughing.

While this dog's owner found the situation funny, I wasn't laughing. Sabrina was going to get it once we got into the car. As I snatched her tiny hand, I was ready to walk out until I saw a familiar face.

For a moment, I was speechless. All I could do was stare. I froze in place until tears of pain and anger appeared. Two years had passed and I could hardly believe my eyes as I looked at the dog's owner. It was Rashad!

He stood with a look of astonishment across his face. Before I made another comment, I grabbed Sabrina's hand and fled out the door.

"What's wrong?" Martina asked as she finished pumping the gas.

"Let's go!" I ordered, getting into the car.

"Alright, let me get my receipt," she said, now becoming concerned.

As I sat in the front seat, I could see him staring at us out the window and he soon disappeared. I was hoping that Martina would return immediately, but she took longer than

I had anticipated. I began to blow the horn. She didn't come out until 15 minutes later.

"What the hell took you so long?" I asked.

"Um, I had to handle somethin'," Martina answered, suspiciously.

Something about her didn't seem right at that moment. I knew that she was hiding something.

"What was it that was so important?" I demanded.

"Nothin' really. Don't worry about it," she said, becoming uncomfortable.

I knew that she was becoming antsy, but I didn't care. I wanted to know what she was up to. As we pulled out of the parking lot, I saw Rashad return to the window. He looked dazed, but he didn't wave and neither did I.

"Who was dat man, Mommy?" Sabrina asked, intrigued.

Rashad continued to stand at the window until we disappeared.

"Nobody important," I answered sadly.

Dominique was at work by the time we arrived home, so I went to bed. For the rest of the week, he tried everything he could to make up for the bad times he put us through. But for some reason, I became detached. My mind was on Rashad.

"What's the matter, baby? You seem out of it?" Dominique asked.

"I'm not feelin' well," I lied but it was partially true. Emotionally, I felt lovesick and confused. Part of me was aching for Rashad for some reason.

"Things are gonna be different for us now," he said while preparing dinner.

As he talked, I sat at the kitchen table, but my mind was somewhere else. I began to drift off. "I've been thinking," he said.

"I'm gonna get all the best kind of help that I can get. I can go to counseling while you continue taking your classes," he said.

Everything he said sounded wonderful. But unfortunately, I wasn't in tune to what he was saying. I didn't care anymore.

"I've thought about something else, too. Maybe we should have a baby. Sabrina could use a playmate," he said, becoming hopeful.

"Here you go, bon appetite," he grinned, placing my favorite dish in front of me.

The smell of barbeque ribs with potato salad and baked beans made my mouth water, but I had to excuse myself.

"I'm not hungry," I said, leaving the table.

Truly, I was starving, but I needed to be alone. I had too many mixed emotions that danced inside my head. I was confused.

"Sweetheart, come back and eat," he begged.

"I'll eat it later," I said, heading toward the bedroom.

I crawled onto the bed and laid on my side, staring at the wall. Should I stay with Dominique or should I leave him for good? I asked myself. I continued staring at the wall, debating whether I loved him or not. Dominique was extremely abusive, but he was an excellent father to Sabrina. I loved how he spent time with her and gave her lots of love and attention something that I never had an idea of since I never had a real father. As I continued thinking of Dominique, thoughts of Rashad soon swarmed into my head.

I suddenly began to envision how my life could have turned out had I stayed with him. Maybe I should have been more demanding two years ago when he discovered that I was pregnant. What if I had chased after him instead of laying on the floor, feeling sorry for myself? Would Sabrina and I have been happier? Or would we have been miserable since he strongly expressed that he wanted no part of it? I suddenly became confused.

Part of me missed Rashad dearly, yet I still hated him. Did this mean that I still loved him? As I remained in deep thought, the phone rang. It was Martina with urgent news. Her desperation suddenly snapped me out of thought.

"It's really important," she urged.

"What is it?" I asked, becoming anxious.

"I have somethin' to give you. But I can't do it over the phone 'cause I know that your man could be listenin' right now. Can you meet me in Dawson's Park?" she asked.

"Martina, what is it? Just tell me," I asked, not wanting to rise out of bed.

"Just meet me at Dawson's Park. Please," she repeated and hung up.

I sat on the bed still holding the receiver. What did she have to show me that was so important now? I thought.

I slipped into a pair of jeans and flip-flops and rushed downstairs to jump into the Lexus inside the garage.

"Where are you going, sweetheart?" Dominique asked while lying on the couch downstairs.

He was sprawled on the couch watching his favorite soccer team on the E-Sports Channel.

"I gotta go to the store," I lied. "Can you watch Sabrina for me?"

"You still didn't eat," he reminded.

"I'll eat it when I come back, OK?" I hurried out before he continued to interrogate or tried to stop me from leaving.

Lately he had been extremely clingy. The other day as we laid in bed, he had a death grip around my waist as I tried to rise out of bed. What was our relationship coming to?

I jumped into my Lexus and met Martina in a flash. She sat on a pair of swings in the playground with her cell phone wedged in her hands. I saw a look of concern across her face.

"Good, you finally made it," she said relieved.

"Martina, you're really startin' to act crazy. What is it?" I asked nervously. I was almost dreading to hear her news.

"Sit down," she offered.

I sat in the swing next to her and waited to hear what she had to say.

"I want you to know that I talked to Sabrina's father."

"What!" I shrieked. "Are you fuckin' serious?"

I couldn't believe what I was hearing.

"Do you remember when we stopped for ice cream that day before we left Virginia Beach?" she asked.

"Yeah."

"Well, there was a guy inside the convenience store. He said that he knew you," Martina said, shifting nervously. "He stopped me, while I was standin' in line to get my receipt. When he approached me, he told me who he was."

"We sat at a booth and we talked. He told me everythin' Cyndi," Martina continued. "He told me the whole story. That's why it took me so long to come out," she explained.

"What an asshole!" I swore. "You shouldn't have talked to him. I don't even know why you wasted your time!" I said angrily.

"Cyndi, I couldn't help it. What was I supposed to do? He just came up to me and started talkin' out of the clear blue," she said. "I don't know what made him wanna talk to me, but I'm thinkin' it's because maybe he saw me talkin' to you outside and put two and two together. Because he got really excited when he discovered that we knew each other."

"Oh wow, it doesn't take a fuckin' genius to figure that shit out. He was watchin' us from the window like a fuckin' idiot!" I snapped.

"What did he say to you?" I asked, now realizing that my mood began to shift.

"Damn!" Martina said, shocked by my comment. "He asked me to give you his number," she started scrolling through her directory in her phone.

"You still haven't told me what he said," I reminded.

"Oh my God, Cyndi, the dude was about to cry. I kid you not," she said. "He told me that you two had some issues that he wanted the two of you to work out," she answered.

"It's none of my business, but I think you should get back with the ol' boy. The dude seemed really sincere," she said. "I'm sure he did some really fucked up shit in the past, but he couldn't be any worse than your Ike Turner man."

"Whatever!" I cried. "If we so-called need to work on our issues, then you ask him why in the hell he decided now to step up and be a fuckin' man after two years. You ask him that!" I fired. "I don't think I'll be talkin' to him, Martina. As far as I know, that nigga's dead to me!"

"Don't you think that sounds a little familiar?" she asked, referring to the situation with David and my mother.

"I don't give a shit," I said through tears.

Martina's eyes began to water, since she felt my emotional pain.

"How long have you known this?" I asked.

"All week."

"Wait a minute, you knew this shit, but you didn't say nothin' to me until now?" I asked.

"I was tryin' to wait for the right time. You seemed really upset that day when you spotted him. I didn't wanna make it worse," she said.

"But then I tried to call you the other day, but Dominique wouldn't put you on the phone and I couldn't reach you on your cell."

"He took it. It was his idea of us spendin' time with no interruptions," I said, rolling my eyes.

"Damn, a prisoner in your own home, wow. Well anyway, I almost didn't wanna tell you. But then I started thinkin'. It's only fair to Sabrina. At least she has somethin' that me and you don't have," Martina said.

"Go ahead and take this number down," she said. "The ball's in your court. You can do whatever you want, but at least you have an opportunity to try to make things right," she advised.

"This is some fucked up shit! I'm confused as fuck!" I cried. "How do I know that he won't hurt me again?" I asked.

"As fucked up as this sounds, it's a chance you take. Love is blind, I know. But put it this way, it's better than sittin' at home gettin' socked around from your man every night, right?" she asked.

"You're right," I said, trying to find courage.

She started to hug me until I flinched. She pulled back as if I were made of ice.

"What's wrong?" she asked.

"Nothin'. I gotta go," I replied, trying to rush off.

"What's on your back, Cyndi?" she asked.

"I gotta go," I repeated, trying to ignore her.

"Cyndi, let me see your back," she begged fearfully.

"OK, look," I said as I turned around sarcastically. "There, are you happy now?"

"Cyndi, stop bullshittin'. Just let me see it. Please," she urged.

"Why?" I asked, now feeling violated. There was no backing out of this situation. Once Martina was concerned with something, she stopped at nothing to investigate.

"Cyndi, I'm your best friend. Come on!"

Glancing around cautiously, I slowly raised the back of my T-shirt and turned the opposite direction to reveal what I regretted. She gasped as she discovered her concern. On my back were bruises and scratches from when Dominique and I fought. There were times when he threw me into a wall or flung an object at me, when he accused me of sleeping with my supervisor. Dominique was so adamant that Keith and I were fooling around, since he found his phone number in my cell phone. My injuries covered my shoulder blades all the way to my tail bone.

"Shit, Cyndi, you let him do this to you?" she gasped.

"Don't tell anyone, OK?" I begged with desperation.

"Girl, what are you thinkin? You're a dead woman stayin' with him!"

"I gotta go," I said.

"Just think about what I said, alright?"

I waved at her, motioning that I heard her as I headed to my car. Immediately as I returned home, I stored Rashad's phone number under a fictitious name, *Dr. Stone*. I didn't feel like battling any more rounds of fist fights with Dominique. Not tonight.

After gobbling down the food that he prepared earlier, I checked on Sabrina and went straight to bed. I had the impression that Dominique was asleep, since he had a tough load of patients at work earlier. But as my head hit the pillow, his arm instantly wrapped me and I couldn't move. This indicated that he laid awake the entire time, waiting for me to return.

Chapter 19

The next morning started with misery as I woke up. He greeted me with such hatred that I would never forget. I sat up in bed trying to get acclimated, as he stood in front of our mirror, adjusting his tie.

"Good mornin', baby," I smiled.

"Who's Taj?" he asked, glaring at me from his reflection.

"What?" I asked, confused.

"Don't play deaf with me. Who's Taj?"

"Where did you hear that name?" I asked, now becoming shocked.

Everything in the room suddenly was at a standstill as I froze.

"Don't worry about where I heard it. It's the fact that he's been on your mind for some reason. Now, I'll ask you again. Who the fuck is Taj?" he yelled.

"I don't know what you're talkin' about," I denied.

Inside, I was terrified. How did he know? As though he were reading my mind, he said, "You said his name in your sleep five times last night."

"No," I denied, shaking my head. This couldn't be true!

"I'm gonna ask you one more time, Cyndi. Who the hell is he?" he raged, now facing me.

"He's just someone I knew from when I was a kid. Don't trip," I said.

"Oh really?" Dominique asked sarcastically. "So your past is catching up with you. Well, I guess that explains this too right?"

As I took a closer look, I saw that he flashed a piece of paper in front of me. It was Rashad's phone number. The day before, I made sure that I stored it inside my phone as a fictitious name before reaching home. Then I threw my cell inside the drawer near my side of the bed. But Dominique obviously must have gone through it while I was asleep. I never heard him stir, since I was so tired. Lately, he'd been quick. Tears now came to my eyes.

"He's Sabrina's father," I answered, trying to fight back the tears.

"I don't believe this shit! You bitch!" he slapped me.

My body fell back against the pillow. I quickly jumped out of bed to run out of the bedroom, until he caught me by my hair.

"Stop! Get off me!" I cried, swinging at him.

"You lied to me, Cyndi. You told me that it was over between you two."

"It was over," I said in between sobs.

"Oh, so you're getting back with him?" he asked resentfully.

"No, that's not what I meant," I said.

"Well, what are you saying, Cyndi? You tell me what's going on," he ordered while hovering over me.

I was now cornered.

"Dominique, don't," I pleaded. "You promised you wouldn't hit me again, remember?"

"And you promised you wouldn't leave me," he said.

I began to cry. "Please let me go."

He backed away and let me rush to the hallway until I realized that he was behind me. I felt him grab my ponytail and slap me again. He shoved me into the wall as I hit my shoulder. When I had the chance, I ran into Sabrina's room.

By this time, she was awake. She sat up in bed waiting for me to scoop her up, so that we could try running for the 100th time. "Mommy!" she cried. I grabbed her as she clung to me.

"So, I guess you're just gonna leave me, huh?" he asked, following us down the hall. "Well, you can forget that. You're not leaving me. You're mine, punta!" he ordered.

I ran to the front door as Sabrina continued to cry. "It's OK, Sabrina, don't cry," I said, trying to calm her.

As I reached the front door, he shoved us and slammed it shut. "Put her down," he commanded.

"Hell no!" I cried.

"Put her down!"

"Leave us alone!" I cried.

"You put her down or I swear you'll never see her again," he threatened.

"You'll have to kill me first."

As he raised his fist, I began to cringe. "OK!" I yelled.

"Put her down!"

I placed Sabrina on the floor and shoved her behind me since we were cornered.

"Go to your room," he commanded her.

Sabrina didn't budge, but continued to cry.

"Sabrina, just go to your room," I pleaded in tears.

She covered her ears, doing what she was told. Once she disappeared, Dominique grabbed me and dragged me to the kitchen.

"Why do you want me to stay when you don't love me?" I asked.

"Shut up!"

"You're hurtin' my arm," I said.

"You haven't felt real pain yet," he sneered.

As I tried to snatch away, his grip tightened, and, his slaps became brutal punches.

"Call him on speaker phone," Dominique said, handing me the cordless.

"No."

"You call lover boy and tell him that it's over, or I will. And believe me, you don't want me to do that," he threatened again.

"I don't care. But I'm not callin' him. We're done, Dominique. I can't live like this anymore," I said, trying to stay strong.

The last thing I wanted to do was break down in front of him. Instead of becoming violent and angrier, he began to snicker. For a moment, it frightened me, until I became upset.

"What the hell is your problem?" I yelled.

Changing emotions again, his face became serious as he stood in front of me. "You honestly think you can make it without me?" he asked.

"I know I can. I don't need you!"

"OK, where are you gonna go? Back to your little 'hood and continue living off your part-time job? You had absolutely nothing when you first met me. What makes you think you can make it now?" he asked.

"I can take care of myself," I said.

"Who's gonna take care of you the way I do?" he asked.

"We don't need you!" I cried.

"You belong to me," he ordered.

As he continued to hover over me, I suddenly spotted a set of carving knives on the counter. As I grabbed one of them, he chased me around the kitchen island. "You can't leave me!" he yelled.

I ran toward the eating area, hoping that I could run out the back door. Previously when we fought, he wanted to be sure the neighbors didn't hear us. He wouldn't dare want to stand out as a minority involved in a domestic disturbance, especially since we lived near his colleagues. But today, I was ready to make our situation well known.

As I was about to grab the door handle, he caught me with one big grip. I suddenly slashed at his leg, trying to aim at his side. He screamed angrily as we began to tussle with the knife. I felt him bang my wrist against the wall, my weapon falling to the floor. Before I knew it, he threw me onto our glass kitchen table.

My whole body fell through the table, feeling every piece of glass in my back as it shattered in a million pieces. I screamed and struggled to get up as he restrained me to the floor. Immediately, I was in so much pain that I could barely move a limb. My T-shirt was soaked with blood. Once again,

Dominique won our battle. Maybe he was right. Maybe I would forever be tied to him.

Instantly, he leaned over me, grabbing my hair as he held the knife against my throat. "You know you're not leaving me, right?" he asked. Anger and rage were still in his eyes. "You're gonna always be mine, right?"

Before I could resist, his grip tightened around my hair. The knife cut deeper into my skin until I agreed against my will. "OK," I sobbed. "I'll stay."

"I can't hear you," he demanded.

"I'll stay!"

He got up and wiped his hands on a towel as though he just cleaned up a small mess and headed out. As he stopped in the hallway, he turned around one last time before leaving.

"You know, if I were you, I would think really hard before walking out or going to the cops. We both know that you're unfit every time you smoke those blunts in the clubs," he said. "Do you really want to lose custody of your daughter? Because sooner or later, it would be your word against mine, and then you tell me who you think they'll believe?" He finally left and headed off to work.

I heard the garage door close and I laid on the floor and cried for the longest time. Thoughts of suicide crossed my mind until I thought of Sabrina. Once I became calm, I packed a small bag and grabbed the other one that was packed previously. I grabbed Sabrina and headed toward our car.

Luckily, she stopped crying but I could tell that she was terrified. I tried reassuring her that we would soon be safe, but I think she sensed that I was still upset. As we pulled out of the garage, one of the neighbors stared at our appearance.

I didn't realize how disoriented we looked until I took a glance in the rear view.

Sabrina and I were still in our pajamas and it was now broad daylight. My hair was astray with a few strands pulled out. My eyes were blood shot and I had welts and bruises on my arms, and scratches at my throat. Remnants of the broken glass were still in my back and my T-shirt that once was white was now bloody red. Sabrina was still dressed in her night gown and pink fuzzy slippers.

"Do you need help, Cyndi?" my neighbor, Mrs. Harper, asked while watering her lawn.

"We'll be fine," I said, ready to drive off.

"Can I take you to a hospital?" she offered.

"I said we'll be OK," I answered defensively after backing out of the driveway.

We pulled off and sped down the road. I wanted her help, but I didn't trust her. This lady always stared at us as though we were criminals and meddled in our business ever since we moved in. She always complained when too many visitors mingled in our yard, or if Sabrina's toys were out in the yard too long. Mrs. Harper even complained about our cookouts and barbeques being too loud, or if too many cars were parked in front of our house. There was always some monotonous issue that she would report about us to our neighborhood association.

Eventually, I realized that being too dark was considered a disturbance for her. For all I knew, Mrs. Harper at this particular moment could have easily wanted to report me since I appeared to be "too emotionally distressed." I didn't need any more trouble from this woman, especially not today. I saw that she finally wore a look of pity, as we left, but I didn't care. Sabrina and I needed to get away.

"Oh my God!" Martina screamed at my appearance.

She took Sabrina from me as I stood on her door- step. I walked to Martina's couch and dropped my bags to the floor. I was tired.

"Let me guess, Dominique again, right?" she asked angrily.

I stared at her teary eyed. I couldn't speak. With Sabrina on her hip, Martina walked to the bathroom and returned with a first-aid kit.

"I really need you to watch Sabrina for me while I go to the ER," I said urgently.

"Fuck that shit, I'm goin' with you. Ooh, I can't believe him!" Martina raged.

As Martina searched for antiseptic in her kit, she spoke to Sabrina. But I knew that her message was directed at me. "Look at your mommy, Sabrina. You're daddy did this to her."

Martina's expression didn't take much convincing this time. I was truly finished with Dominique for good. Sabrina became amazed.

"Daddy?" she asked, surprised.

"You see, Sabrina," Martina began, "you have a good daddy and a bad daddy. But your bad daddy did this to her."

"Martina, stop!" I insisted.

"What? I'm explainin' somethin' to her. She needs to know this."

"No she doesn't. I don't want her to have any more bad memories than what we already have," I said.

"It's too late for that," Martina said.

"Look, are you done? 'Cause right now, I'm ready to go," I huffed.

"Whatever," Martina answered, impatiently.

Both of us were now becoming frustrated with each other due to my ongoing situation with Dominique.

"Hey Sabrina, do you wanna go watch cartoons?" she asked, trying to change the subject.

"Yeah! I want Cartoon Network!" Sabrina cheered.

While Martina was getting Sabrina settled, I went into the bathroom to change into clothes. I wanted to come out of those bloody pajamas and take care of my throbbing face. I had only expected to see a few scratches on my face.

But instead, as I stared at my reflection, I saw a swollen eye, a bruised cheek and a cut lip. Damn! I was almost afraid to look at myself. My back was severely scratched with a few pieces of glass still remaining. The last time Dominique and I fought, I suffered a swollen jaw.

After becoming remorseful, Dominique wanted to arrange for a plastic surgeon to correct my jaw. But luckily, some of my inflammation went down within a few days. But today, my injuries wouldn't heal that easily. As I dabbed my face with a damp cloth, I started to cry. Martina came in and hugged me.

"You gotta leave him, Cyndi. He's not worth it. Please tell me you're leavin' him?" she begged.

"I am. I really am," I sniffled.

Once I became calm, she helped me clean my scratches and applied ointment. Just when we were about to call the police, Devon spotted me.

"What the fuck happened?" he asked, alarmed.

"Don't worry about it, Devon. We got it covered," Martina said, trying to keep him from becoming agitated.

"Was it bitch-ass Dominique?" Devon demanded.

"It doesn't matter," I said, applying an icepack to my swollen eye.

"It doesn't matter?" Devon asked angrily. "You tell me who did this to you, Cyndi. Tell me!"

"Devon, let it go. He's not worth it," Martina said.

"Fuck that! I don't care how much money that nigga has or how many attorneys he's got. I betcha he could still use an ass whoopin'! That nigga runs his mouth too much anyway," Devon yelled.

"We're callin' the police right now," I informed.

"Fuck the police. They ain't gon' do shit. They're only gonna let him go 'cause he's got money," Devon stated.

"Devon, just let it go!" Martina yelled.

I hated that I got him involved now. Maybe I should've fled straight to the hospital. But that meant I would have had to take Sabrina with me. And I didn't want her to be sitting inside the hospital for several hours. She was still hungry since we hadn't had breakfast yet.

"Where is he?" Devon asked.

"Don't worry about it," I said.

"Tell me where he is!" Devon repeated.

"Hello, I'd like to report an assault!" Martina yelled into the phone.

I knew that she was purposely raising her voice to get Devon's attention. It was her way of informing him that law enforcement was on the phone.

"Is he at work?" Devon asked, ignoring her tone.

I didn't have to answer. Devon was already out the door.

"Don't worry about it. I gotta go handle somethin' anyway," he said storming out.

"Devon, no!" Martina cried, trying to chase after him.

But it was too late; he started his car and was gone.

"Fuck!" she screamed.

Sabrina began to cry until I went to pick her up.

"If the cops pull him over now, he's done. We're still in the process of gettin' his case expunged," she said.

Damn! All this was my fault, I thought.

Chapter 20

Shortly after Devon left, the police arrived. One officer, who appeared to be in his late 30s, jotted information down in his report. The other, who was middle-aged, began to snap photos of my injuries. I gave a statement describing every detail of how our argument started, also back tracking to the time our domestic disputes began earlier in our relationship. As I spoke with the officers, I became anxious, fearing that Dominique would try to take Sabrina since he made several threats if I ever tried to leave.

"You don't understand," I said fearfully. "My boyfriend makes tons of money, so I know he's capable of gettin' custody of my daughter. He's always sayin' that he can prove that I'm unfit."

"Ma'am, I seriously doubt that he has that much power now that we've created a paper trail about his pattern of domestic assault," the younger officer said. "But if you're still having doubts, it wouldn't hurt to take that issue up with child protective services," he said. "They can give you all the insight that you need."

"In the meantime, you can best believe that we plan on taking action on taking him in," the other officer stated.

"We see this type of situation happen a lot in domestic situations," they explained. "A lot of times, the victim is usually afraid to leave or press charges. But I can't urge you enough to get checked at the hospital and to seek social services as soon as possible."

"Was there any harm done to your daughter, ma'am?" the younger officer asked suspiciously. I had the impression that he assumed I was withholding additional information.

"No," I said. "Believe it or not, he's actually good to my daughter, but treats me like shit," I said in tears.

"Ma'am, we're going to do everything we can to protect you. But please get admitted to a hospital. And if anything else comes up, please don't hesitate to give us a call," they urged while handing me their cards.

"I just want him locked up. Please lock his ass up," I said, ready to take action.

"We will do everything we can, ma'am" the middle-aged officer stated.

After signing a few forms, Martina walked them out to their car. She made it clear to them that she was willing to work against Dominique in my favor. "Oh, we'll be in touch, alright. You can best believe that," she said angrily.

As soon as the officers left, they drove straight to the medical center to arrest Dominique. Luckily, they had just missed Devon 20 minutes earlier. He was already on his way home from their confrontation.

Martina and I drove to the ER and ran into one of my effeminate ex-co-workers, Jeremy. Jeremy and I used to work together as health aides at a nursing home facility. He and I became friends since he had similar characteristics as my old friend, Antoinette. As Jeremy entered my examination room with his clipboard, he gave us the details of what happened. "Oh my God, let me tell you somethin', girl," he said.

As Martina and I sat in the room waiting for my nurse to appear, he stepped behind the curtain with us. He glanced around cautiously so that others wouldn't overhear his usual gossip. "Honey, your boy got his ass knocked the fuck out," he whispered as his blue eyes dazzled in amazement.

"What do you mean?" I asked.

"I just got a text from my man. You know he just started workin' at that medical center where your boy works, right?" he informed.

Before we could answer, Jeremy continued to give us his usual scoop.

"I don't know what went down before, girl. But what I do know is that Dr. Sanchez," he said, referring to Dominique, "steps out of his car in the parkin' garage and, out of nowhere, this dude shows up and starts beatin' his ass all over the place!"

"Are you serious?" Martina asked, laughing.

I couldn't believe what I was hearing.

"As a heart attack, girl," he said, as he rolled his neck and snapped his fingers.

"Well, what happened after that?" I asked, wanting more details.

Jeremy glanced around again and continued speaking more discreetly with us.

"Ol' dude got his face smashed in and I think his arm got fucked up, too, girl."

"Wait a minute, you're tellin' me that all this shit went down and nobody did nothin'? What about the security cameras?" I asked, still in shock.

"All that was covered up girl," he said. "Let's just say that ol' boy who stomped the doctor's ass kinda had connections with my man who works in security."

"Wait a minute, what kinda connections?" Martina asked skeptically. I could already tell that she was now dreading to hear of her man becoming a DL brotha.

"Oh girl, it ain't nothin' like that. Don't even trip," Jeremy said, rolling his eyes. "But anyway, your man paid my boyfriend a few extra dollars so he could turn off the cameras and walk away momentarily," Jeremy smirked.

"Come on now. I ain't buyin' that shit," Martina said skeptically.

"I'm serious, girl. The dude who beat up the doctor kept yellin' at him about smackin' on some woman and for fuckin' up his job," Jeremy explained.

"Wait a minute, what happened at his job?" I asked, not understanding what he meant at this point.

Yet, Martina had an idea. "So, that explains why he wanted to beat his ass."

"What the fuck are you talkin' about?" I asked.

Martina now became upset. "A couple months ago, Devon got in trouble at work. He was set up."

"What do you mean?" I asked.

"Do you remember that time when he locked you in your bedroom?" Martina reminded.

"Yeah."

"Well, that night when Devon left for work, I had to get him outta jail. He got arrested for supposedly carryin' a concealed weapon. I know nobody else could have put that shit on him but your boy," Martina fired. "Only because he was paranoid that you and Devon had somethin' goin' on. He came to our house one day flippin' out over that shit and tried to start a fight with Devon."

"What?" I shrieked, now feeling stupid. All this time, Dominique was trying everything he could to sabotage my support system with Martina and Devon. But in reality, I had no clue.

"There's no way that I can ever prove it, but I know it was him, 'cause that day when I called the cops on his ass, I remember Dominique sayin' shit about how he was gonna fuck our lives up," Martina continued. She spoke angrily while discussing every detail.

"Devon's backpack supposedly went off at the sensors' when he was comin' in to work. That's when they searched his bag and they found a gun that mysteriously appeared," Martina explained.

"Luckily, the prints didn't match on the gun, so he got off. But that's beside the point. We're still tryin' to straighten that shit out," she said.

"I'm so sorry," I said, now feeling like a dumb ass.

"Dominique's a sick motha fucka, Cyndi. I don't know what else to tell you," Martina stated harshly.

Jeremy stood listening to us, amazed. "Wow, that's some crazy ass shit!"

"Are you alright?" he finally asked, suddenly remembering my situation.

"Don't worry about me," I said, trying to fight back tears.

After trying to cheer me up with more funny gossip on his new job, Jeremy gave me a hug and quickly slipped out with his clipboard.

"Keep ya head up, girl. It's gonna be alright," he said before stepping out. Jeremy soon hurried off to continue his discharge procedure duties. Shortly afterwards, my doctor and nurse appeared.

After answering a series of questions during my examination, I was sent to the X-ray unit. Once they found that no bones were broken, I was given stitches for the cuts on my back. My physician prescribed an ointment for my deep scratches and jotted notes in his chart. Shortly before being discharged, the doctor disappeared but my nurse remained in the room. She offered a card with several hotlines and agencies to call.

"You don't have to live in fear anymore," she said, sincerely.

"I hope you're right," I said.

"At times, it's hard in the beginning, but I can assure you that once you get your support system set up, you'll be in good hands. Just stay strong. It's gonna be alright," she advised while patting my shoulder.

"So what you gonna do now?" Martina asked once we returned from the ER.

"I'm gonna leave. For good," I answered.

"Do you know where you're goin'? If not, you know you and Sabrina always got a home here with us," Martina offered.

"We can't. Not this time," I said, sadly. "This is the very first place that Dominique will look to find me. He always finds me here."

"Well not anymore. He's in jail now."

"It doesn't matter. Dominique's got all kinds of crazy connections with his income. For all I know, he could be payin' his attorney top dollar right now just to get out," I said warily. "I have to be a step ahead of him this time."

"OK, so where you goin'?" Martina repeated.

I could tell she was concerned with my plan B.

"I'm goin' to a shelter. I called them before we left the hospital and spoke with an intake counselor. She says I can come in tonight. I think we'll be safer there for now," I answered.

"Wow," Martina said, amazed. "Good luck to you for real. I'm gonna miss you guys."

We began to hug each other, already feeling a sense of farewell. "Just remember that if things don't work out, you two are still welcome here," she said.

"Thanks Martina."

Sabrina entered the room with her toys as she stared at us helplessly. I picked her up and kissed her adorable face. "We're gonna be OK now," I assured her with a hug.

"No more bad daddy?" she asked.

"No," I smiled. "No more bad daddy."

"I gotta get ready for work," Martina said, now realizing the time. We had been gone for four hours and it was now turning to the afternoon.

"Alright I'll just run home and get a few things," I said.

"You need me to go with you?" Martina asked.

"No, you've done more than enough. But you can watch Sabrina if you don't mind. I'll only be a few minutes," I said.

"Alright."

I headed toward the front door until I stopped. "Hey Martina!" I called.

"What?" she stood in the hallway.

"I want you to thank Devon for beatin' Dominique's ass for me."

"Most definitely," she laughed.

I closed her door and drove home. I was ready to leave Dominique for good. Part of me was sad that we couldn't work out. I really loved him. I would miss the good times that we did have and our comfortable, luxurious house. Yet, I was afraid of him. I couldn't continue to live in fear anymore. Why did this have to happen? Was I destined to never find the love that I truly deserved?

As I walked into the house, I stared at the remnants of our war from that morning. The curtains were still drawn, which made the house dark, but I could still see everything. Pictures of our so-called family memories were now scattered on the floor. Clothes were thrown everywhere, and our kitchen table was shattered.

I saw small spots of dried blood that remained on the kitchen floor from where I fell. The pillows from the living room furniture were tussled. Everything was a wreck due to our brutal fight. I walked past the mess and headed toward the bedroom to pack another bag. As I entered our bedroom, I heard sobbing that was muffled from the walk-in closet. Who in the hell would be here at a time like this? I thought.

I opened the closet door and discovered Dominique! He sat on the floor in a depressive slump with a bandaged nose and swollen lip. I couldn't help but shriek at his appearance.

"What the hell are you doin' here?" I screamed.

"I wanted to see you," he said sadly.

"You can't. It's too late for that," I said, heading toward the front door.

"Cyndi, wait! Come back!" he called, running after me.

"Get away from me!" I yelled, now breaking into a sprint.

"Cyndi, please," he begged as he caught up with me.

He clung to me tightly, as if I would slip out of his fingers instantly.

"Get off me! Get off!" I cried, trying to swing at him.

Dominique continued to restrain me.

"You're not supposed to be here!" I yelled.

"I needed to see you, Cyndi. I love you," he said. His grip became tighter.

By this time, I was fed up. Nothing he said would convince me of coming back. We were finished.

"You call that love?" I asked sarcastically. "After what you did to me? We're done, Dominique, it's over."

"Don't say that!" he cried. "Please don't say that. I know you don't want to throw away what we have."

"No, you did that Dominique. You threw away what we had a long time ago. I was just too blind to see it," I said in tears.

"Please don't leave me, Cyndi. I want to work on us," he urged.

"There is no us," I stated.

"Don't say that!"

I tried to break out of his embrace. This scenario was starting to get old.

"Please don't leave me, Cyndi. I love you. I don't know what I'd do without you."

"Stop!" I cried.

"I can't live without you. And I won't let you live without me," he said, firmly. Dominique suddenly gave me an expression that I'd never seen before as he stared intently into my eyes.

"You know I love you," he said, trying to kiss me.

I began to resist. I didn't want his swollen lips on me anymore at this point.

"Dominique, don't," I resisted.

"Come on baby," he urged.

"I said stop!"

"Oh, so I'm not good enough for you anymore, but you can get with Sabrina's father?" he accused.

No matter how much I resisted, he continued to be aggressive. He suddenly shoved me into the wall and stared at me intently again.

"You're not leaving me, Cyndi. You're mine," he ordered. "I took you out of that 'hood and let you come stay with me. Then I put you in the pent-house and let you splurge on my credit cards for your little designer clothes and this is how you wanna treat me?" he yelled.

"You wanna leave me after I took care of your daughter when her own daddy wouldn't step up to the plate? You wanna leave me? After all I've done for you?" he raged. "You're not going anywhere. We're a family and we're gonna work through this."

"You're not my family, Dominique. And I don't need you. I got someplace I gotta be," I said, trying to peel out of his grip.

"Where are you going?" he asked.

"Don't worry about where I'm goin'!" I snapped.

"You're going to see your little boyfriend, right?"

"Whatever."

"What's his name?" Dominique probed.

"Get outta my face," I ordered.

"Tell me who he is. Is it Devon?"

"Get outta my face!" I repeated.

"Did you suck his dick? Was he better than me?" Dominique continued.

At this point, Dominique was on one of his rages again. No matter what I said to deny or avoid his accusations, he only became more upset. Eventually, I became fed up. There was no point in trying to talk with him anymore.

"Yeah, we got that shit on You Tube. His crew cam-corded the whole thing. You wanna fuckin' watch?" I asked rudely.

Dominique slapped me hard, which happened so quickly. My head whipped back so hard that I almost blacked out. Instantly, I pounced on him and began to punch his face. Dominique and I scuffled as we fell to the floor.

As he grabbed my hair, I quickly pulled a Mike Tyson move and bit his ear all the way through the gristle. I didn't care anymore. If he wanted to take me down, we were going together. I grabbed the cordless phone that had fallen to the floor.

"Put the phone down," he ordered.

"Fuck you!" I cried.

"Put it down!" he now had my arm pinned behind my back. One wrong movement could instantly break it.

"OK, OK!" I said, giving up. "What do you want me to do?"

"Where's Sabrina?" he asked.

"I'm not fuckin' tellin' you!"

He started to raise my head by my ponytail, threatening to slam my face into the floor until I gave in.

"She's at Martina's!"

"Let's go get her," he said.

"I'll go pick her up," I said, quickly trying to think of a plan.

"No, we're going together," he ordered.

"OK, Dominique, whatever you say," I obliged.

Chapter 21

*D*ominique had me drive his car as he sat in the passenger seat with a nine millimeter gun in his lap. I never knew he had had a stash of unregistered guns inside a safe downstairs in our basement. As we drove, he watched every move that I made. If I needed to use my cell phone, he dialed the number. If I flashed a turning blinker incorrectly, he immediately had me correct it. At this point, I realized that he was right. There was no leaving Dominique. He was too quick for me to find a way for me to survive.

"OK, we're going inside to get Sabrina and then we're coming right out. So don't try to pull any funny shit," he said, forcing me to open my door once we reached Martina's. His gun was now lodged at my side.

I was sure my intestines were going to be spilled out on the car seats at any moment.

"You know what, how about you let me get her while you wait here? I don't want you and Devon to be fightin' again," I said, trying to plot against him. "So just let me get everything, alright?"

"Hurry up!" he snapped. "And I'm fucking serious, no funny shit."

"Alright," I said, cautiously.

Martina answered the door with a confused expression.

"Are you alright?" she asked.

"Call the police," I whispered, closing her front door. "He's here."

"Who, Dominique?"

"Yes! He was at home when I got there and then we had another fight. He made me drive here to get Sabrina and he's got a gun!" I said, now freaking out. Call the police! Please!"

"Ah, hell naw. I'm 'bout to get my glock!" she raged. "Fuck that nigga!"

As she dialed 911, I went into Martina's bedroom and picked up Sabrina. I sat her inside the closet with her toys to hide. This was my only way of providing protection for her. What if he broke one of the windows and came into the bedroom to leave with her? I couldn't let that happen!

"Now, be quiet," I told her, "because there's a big, evil dragon standin' outside our castle. So you gotta protect the princess. Can you do that for me?" I asked, trying to create a make-believe game to engage her. I didn't want her to be afraid.

"Yeah," she smiled, hugging her doll.

I shushed her and softly closed the door.

I suddenly heard Dominique at the front door.

"What the hell is taking so long, Cyndi? Open the door!"

"I already called the cops, but it ain't over yet," Martina said psychotically. She had hatred and anger radiating from her face that I had never seen before.

"Well, they need to hurry their asses up. This shit is crazy," I said nervously.

"Open the door, Cyndi," he commanded, now pounding on the windows with his gun.

"You got exactly five seconds to get away from my house, bitch!" Martina raged. She had just pulled back her clip, ready to fire at any moment.

Before we knew it, we finally heard sirens coming from three patrol cars. "Drop the weapon and place your hands behind your head! Now!" we heard an officer order from a bull-horn.

"Drop the gun, Martina," I urged.

The last thing we needed was for her to go down with him. It took a couple of seconds for her to snap out of her revenge mode. But eventually, she placed the safety clip back on and tossed it underneath her couch.

Dominique became enraged as he smashed one of the windows. "You fucking bitch! Pay back is a bitch, let me tell you that!" he threatened.

As they placed him into the patrol car, I finally had the courage to step outside. I wanted to be sure that I saw him get taken away. By this time, every neighbor was out, watching the entire commotion.

"It's really over this time, ma'am. I'm sorry that it had to come to this. But now, he can't hurt you anymore," the officer said.

"He was supposed to be arrested earlier. What the hell happened?" I cried.

"He was detained earlier for a booking. But shortly afterwards, he was released with a restraining order. He was told not to report to the premises until you moved out," the officer explained. "But after this incident, we now can charge him for violating his restraining order and having a deadly weapon. You should be OK now."

"Are you alright?" another officer asked.

"I'll be a lot better if you take his ass away for good. I don't wanna see him anymore," I said.

"You'll be much safer now, miss," they swore.

"No, I'll be safer when you get all his guns."

"Guns?" both officers became puzzled.

"Yeah, go check out our place. He's got a stash of every gun that gets imported here," I informed.

After completing another police report, I lead the officers to my home and revealed Dominique's secret stash. He had everything from military guns to nine millimeters and silencers. All that time, I had never realized just how much danger Sabrina and I were in until now. Thank God we were finally getting out!

"You can trust and believe that he won't be coming anywhere near you now. We definitely got something on him," the officers replied.

I wanted to feel relieved, but I couldn't. My body continued to tremble as I watched them continue their investigation.

It took a great deal to convince me that we were safe. I remained paranoid and nervous several weeks after Dominique's arrest. At times, I had nightmares of seeing his angry face and feeling his brutal punches. Or sometimes, I would hallucinate and think I would see him standing nearby flashing his gun. Dominique was gone, but unfortunately my horrid memories would never go away. Sabrina and I eventually admitted ourselves into a shelter.

It was a program where victims of domestic violence could receive counseling and transitional services. Toward the end of the program, victims would get assistance with job seeking and finding permanent housing. During our transition, Sabrina attended a children's therapy program and I attended individual and group therapy. For the first few weeks, I was terrified. It took me a while to adjust until I truly felt safe. Several weeks passed and I began to physically heal, but struggled with emotional wounds. To complicate things further, I discovered I was pregnant.

So much chaos had occurred that I hadn't noticed the symptoms until I missed two menstrual cycles. It was shortly after entering the program. I sat in the bathroom stall and I cried as I read, the positive results of the pregnancy test. There was a time when Dominique talked about us having a child together. He once told me that he saw his children twice a year. But toward the end of our relationship, I learned that he was not permitted to see his children from his first marriage. And, his second wife had experienced a miscarriage. Therefore, both losses had made him want to start another family, yet I wasn't ready.

I sat inside the stall crying and realizing that I never picked up my refill of the Nuva Ring. So many problems had occurred between Dominique and me that I had forgotten to maintain my physical health. A few months earlier, I probably would have been more hopeful about this pregnancy. Dominique always swore that he would become a better father if I gave him another chance. But today I had mixed feelings. Two days later, I scheduled an appointment for an abortion. I knew that Dominique would have been furious if he'd known about this, but I didn't care. I wanted him out of my life. After completing the procedure, I was haunted with guilt, wondering if my unborn child's spirit would be angry with me.

I remembered the time I encountered my near-death experience years before after the brawl with Brittney. I stood in an open pasture and saw the figure of Sabrina and another child at a stream. During that time, I was confused, not fully understanding why I saw two small figures. But now, I realized that both figures were my children. Sabrina was the child who survived, whereas the other child remained behind, since I cut his life short. Part of me was grief stricken, yet I had to move forward with my life. There was no turning back at this point. Sabrina and I needed to heal. I continued with my recovery and months passed.

Sabrina was making progress with healthy coping mechanisms and I was striving for new independence for us. I wanted her to be safe. During this time, I kept in contact with my mother. I told her the ugly details of Dominique's abuse, which made her upset.

"I should've been there for you," she said sadly.

At one of my visitations with her, she gave me a web-site address to look up. "Check this web-site out when you get home," she said with a grim expression.

When I explored the site, I discovered more history on Dominique. He had had a criminal history of domestic violence with both wives. His first spouse fled the country with their children, which explained why he was denied contact with them. His second wife was beaten so severely that she lost their child during her second trimester. I was horrified as I read the reports.

No wonder! I thought. How stupid was I to believe everything that he said?

As I continued to read his rap sheet, I learned that his wives and I all had one thing in common. All of us were women who were younger and needy. His first wife wanted a visa and his second wife was a previous patient that he treated. She was transitioning from a homeless shelter, until he offered her a luxurious home with a violent marriage. After learning more about Dominique's history, I swore that I would never put Sabrina in harm's way again.

If we had to continue living without a male figure, that was fine. There would be no more fist fights and running for safety. As I continued contact with my mother, Sabrina sometimes attended, which often brought tears to my mom's eyes.

"She's beautiful," my mother said, mesmerized.

"Of course, she gets it from her mama," I said, laughing.

"I see myself through you," she said one day while staring at me with a dreamy gaze. "You're a good mother, Cyndi."

"No, I'm not," I denied, on the verge of tears. At times, I felt that I failed because of the bad choices I made with Dominique.

"Yes, you are. Don't ever doubt yourself. You're very brave and you're strong. Stay that way," she said firmly.

"I'll try," I said.

Through our visits and sharing our feelings and pain, my mother and I's connection grew over time. Somehow, despite the absence of each other in our early years, we were bonded. I hoped that Sabrina and I would have this same type of connection as she grew up.

Chapter 22
2010

Four years had passed and my life was better. Sabrina and I were finally living in peace and she was happy. Now that I was 24, I was in the final year of my program at the University of Phoenix. I was completing a paid internship at an urgent care center and studying for my nurse's license. Once I passed the exam, I could become a certified health administrator. My biggest dream was to oversee a pediatric unit at a hospital. Sabrina was now six years old.

She was in the first grade and aced every spelling test she took. I was so proud of how quickly she retained what she learned in her class. At times, I thought about encouraging her to compete in the school's spelling bee since she was such a gifted speller. My mother had been released from her treatment program. She now lived in a small apartment and worked first shift at a residential facility for homeless women. A couple nights a week, she volunteered at group homes and youth facilities. My mother enjoyed sharing her testimony to young women and teen girls. It was her way of preventing other girls from following in her footsteps.

I knew that my mother was disappointed with her past decisions. But I was proud of the current progress that she had made. And I was thrilled that our relationship was started and improving every day.

"Twenty four years is a long time to make up," she would say at times.

"We're not gonna worry about that," I said as we sat inside a food court at the mall.

Sabrina was excitedly digging through her shopping bags of new shoes that my mom had just bought her. "Thanks Grandma!" she cried.

"You're welcome, baby. Now eat up before your mom makes me take those shoes back," my mother joked.

Sabrina quickly spooned a mouthful of stir-fried rice into her mouth as we laughed. These times were good.

"Mommy?" Sabrina asked, skipping beside me.

"Yes, sweetheart," I said as we walked in the park one day.

"Why are we at the park today?"

I had to think a minute, since I wasn't sure myself.

"Well," I started. "Martina said that she had a surprise for us."

"Oh," she replied, continuing her skipping.

As we walked to a picnic table, I became inquisitive and suspicious. What was Martina really up to? I thought. She called me at the last minute the previous day, insisting that we should meet at Dawson's Park.

"I hope it's a puppy, because uncle Devon promised he'd buy me a Chihuahua," she said excitedly.

"You're kiddin' right?" I asked.

"Nope!" she sang.

"Hmm, that sounds like Devon alright," I said, thinking out loud. He's always spoiled her ever since the day she was born.

"Yeah, you made it!" Martina cheered as we approached her.

"Auntie Martina!" Sabrina cried. She ran toward her with open arms.

"Hey girl, come here. Give me a hug," Martina said. "You're gettin' so big!"

I watched them embrace like two sisters.

"Where's my dog?" Sabrina asked.

"Uh, in your mom's paycheck," Martina answered, giving me a skeptical look.

"Can we mommy? Can we?" she begged.

"Are you crazy!" I shrieked. "No we can't get a dog. Now go play," I gestured toward a set of swings.

"Well, what can I say, Cyndi? You did good," Martina said as we watched her run toward the playground.

"You can start by first tellin' me what this is all about. I put my studyin' down just so I could get here on time. So what's up?" I demanded.

There was no telling what Martina had up her sleeve these days.

"Really?" she asked, playing dumb.

"Come on Martina, you blew up my phone with 50 million text messages to remind me about today. Then you begged me to bring Sabrina. She's supposed to be at her spellin' club right now," I said.

"Oh, my bad," Martina apologized, smirking.

"You had me runnin' around like a chicken with his head cut off tryin' to beat that crazy traffic," I continued. "So whatever it is, this better be good."

"OK, OK," she said, sighing. "Take a deep breath, you're in for a big surprise."

"OK, what?" I asked.

"Somebody's here to see you," she said.

"Who?" I asked nervously.

I wasn't in the mood for meeting with professional people. Nor was I dressed in my best attire. Today I was wearing a pair of ragged jeans with a wife beater and flip-flops. My hair was pulled up into a sloppy ponytail inside a large clip. I was tired and just rushed to change out of my work uniform from earlier.

"Damn, Martina, you could've told me. Now I need to change," I complained.

"Calm down, don't worry. He'll like you the way you are. Trust me," she convinced.

"He?" I asked. "Martina, what's goin' on?"

"Oh shit, I said too much," she said. "OK, he's on his way now."

"You haven't told me nothin' Martina. What the hell is goin' on?" I asked impatiently.

Before she could answer, we were interrupted. "Hello ladies," a voice greeted.

I turned around and, once again, was facing Rashad.

"Hey, what's up?" she greeted with a one-armed hug.

Before I could stop her, Martina scampered away.

"OK, gotta go. Call me later Cyndi, so we can catch up," she said.

While Rashad wasn't looking, I explicitly lipped, "I'll fuckin' kill you!"

She continued smirking and ran off. Before she left the park, she walked to Sabrina and handed her a $20 bill.

"Here's a small payment for your dog," Martina said.

"Thanks!" Sabrina cried as she hugged her.

I stared at them until Rashad interrupted my trance.

"Hello Cyndi," he said.

I spun around and faced him. "What the hell are you doin' here?"

"I came to see you. Damn, you look good!" he smiled.

"Why?" I demanded.

"I wanted to see you."

"You need to get the fuck outta my face. And I need to smack Martina for settin' this whole thing up, 'cause I don't wanna see your ass for real!" I raged. "Get outta here!"

No matter how hostile and angry I was, Rashad remained calm and remorseful.

"It wasn't Martina's idea for real. It was mine. I called and blew up her phone for two weeks, until she finally called me back and we talked about it," he said.

"I asked her to contact you so that we could talk. At first I was goin' to show up at your job on your lunch break, but I figured that wouldn't be a good idea," he continued.

"Wow, you did one thing right!" I snapped. "I suppose you should earn a metal for that, right? But we don't need you. I don't want you and I don't want you around me. So get to steppin'!"

"You have every right to hate me. I deserve it. But I want to make it right. That's why I'm here now," he said.

"What do you want?"

"I want to love you. I want to be in your life again," he said sincerely.

"What?" I yelled. "Get outta my face, Rashad," I shoved him and started to walk away.

"Cyndi," he gently seized my arm. "I know I fucked up. That's why I'm here. I flew all the way out here just so I could see you. I've been doin' a lot of thinking."

"Since when?" I asked.

"Since that time we saw each other at the convenience store," he answered.

"Are you fuckin' serious? Why in the hell didn't you say somethin' then?" I raged.

"To be honest with you, I wasn't sure what to say," he said.

"So you wait for four years to fuckin' come tell me this shit?" I cried, now on the verge of tears.

"I'm sorry," he apologized. "Now that I see her, I realize that I missed out on a lot. But I wanna make up for it." He became teary eyed.

"You missed out alright. But we made it. We don't need you!"

"When I saw you in the store, I have to say I was shocked. I still remember that day when you told me you were pregnant. I punked out. I wasn't ready, but I should've been a man. I should've stepped up to the plate," he said.

"When I walked out of that apartment that day, I thought you left and got rid of it. I really thought you had an abortion and went on with your life. I've always regretted that," he expressed.

"But then, when I saw my daughter for the first time, I knew she was mine. I just knew it. There was somethin' about her that told me that we were connected. She was beautiful. She had your smile and your feisty personality. I took a look at her and realized how much of her life I missed. I'm so sorry Cyndi," he apologized trying to hug me.

I pulled away and shoved him hard. I couldn't let him see me cry. "Why are you doin' this when you only care about yourself? Why do you wanna do that to us?"

"I wanna love you Cyndi. Please let me," he begged. Tears flooded his eyes.

"You only cared about your modelin' career. You made that clear from day one. Please don't do that to us, Rashad. Sabrina doesn't need you in her life when she's doin' so well," I sneered.

"What can I say? I was an asshole. I was young and dumb, but people change. I want the two of you to be in my life. I really do."

Part of me wanted to forgive him, but I couldn't. It took me so long to emotionally reach the place where I was. I couldn't go through it again not another emotional roller-coaster. And Sabrina definitely didn't deserve to go through it either.

"So what happened with your career? Shouldn't you be posin' up beside Tyson in the Man of the Month calendar or tryin' out for movies right now?" I asked, trying to change the subject. As I calmed a bit waiting for his answer, I thought about the fact that he came out all this way to see us.

"I got burnt out. My image only lasted for so long until the demand changed," Rashad explained. "Soon, my agent stopped bookin' me gigs and work became slow. And so did the money.

"I lost everything. My home, my car, my friends and most of all my pride. I gained 40 pounds and turned to the bottle. Maybe it's good that I wasn't in your life then. Because I was a mess. I wasn't the man that you fell in love with," he said.

"I don't think you'll ever be the man I once loved," I stated.

"I hope that one day I can be," he softly said.

"So what are you doin' with yourself now?" I asked.

"I'm now in ATL doin' marketin' and some film directin'. I go out and recruit models and also consult for Warner Management, the company run by Malcolm Jamal Warner. I had a chance to meet him one time at a jazz event. He was incredible," Rashad answered.

"And while I was in college majorin' in communications and media, I attended a 12 step program and went to AA. I'm still in Atlanta, but I'm about to move to New Mexico since it's not been hit as hard by the recession. I'm seriously tryin' to make connections on the West Coast," he said excitedly.

"That's impressive," I replied sarcastically.

"I understand that you went through some dark times too. I'm sorry that he put you through hell. No woman should ever have to go through that," he empathized.

"I don't know what you're talkin' about," I denied.

Nobody but Martina could have told him the shit that went down with Dominique.

"We don't have to talk about it if you don't want to. I understand," he tried placing his hand on my shoulder.

"It's none of your fuckin' business!" I snapped.

"But it is my business. I wasn't there for you when you needed me and I'm sorry. But I love you and Sabrina and want to be there for you now," he offered.

"I'm so sick of you dudes comin' around with your bullshit apologies and broken promises. I'm done!"

"I have a lot of apologies, but I don't have broken promises. Not this guy," he said sincerely.

"Go to hell!" I fired.

I expected him to walk away, but instead he didn't!

"You were physically abused your entire life, Cyndi. All you wanted was a family to love and protect you, but you never got that chance when you grew up in foster care. And then you met me, but I didn't give that to you either," he said sadly.

I struggled with fighting back the tears. Why did he have to go down memory lane?

"I should've taken the time to learn about your situation but I didn't find out until it was too late. And then you met your monster ex-boyfriend who tricked you with false love and punches and beatin's. Little did I know that he was markin' your beautiful body up with scratches and bruises," he said.

"Just stop it, OK?" I ordered.

"Damn! You didn't deserve that shit Cyndi, when all I had to do was be a man and step up. Then you wouldn't have had to turn to your abusive boyfriend for love. I really fucked up, Cyndi. I'm sorry," he tried to embrace me again.

At first I threw angry punches at his chest, making up for the many days of emotional pain that he put me through. Rashad stood in place and accepted them, until I finally broke down and cried. He grabbed my fists as I was about to give him my final blow. Soon, he pulled me toward him and embraced me tightly as I clung to him. At first, I wanted to pull away. I hated that he was seeing me in this vulnerable state. Instead of releasing me, he gently grabbed my face. Rashad gave me that lingering kiss that my lips had longed for, for so many years. His lips softly caressed mine, as his biceps wrapped tighter around me. His embrace became soothing.

"I should've been there for you, but I wasn't. Instead I was self-centered and backed away. I'm sorry, Cyndi. I'm sorry for everything."

"It's too late," I said in between sobs.

"No, it's not. Please let me in," he pleaded.

I stood in front of him and tried to compose myself when Sabrina called out in excitement. "Mommy, look!"

I watched her flip out of her swing and land on her feet after completing a somersault. Her long, braided pigtails flared out as did her pink sundress that revealed *Little Mermaid* underwear underneath. But she didn't care. Sabrina stood waiting for her applause as she beamed with pride.

"Excellent! Next time do flips when you're wearin' shorts. I told you about that!" I lectured.

"She's really talented," Rashad remarked.

"She wants to take gymnastics so bad. I keep tellin' her that I'll take her dependin' on her grades this year," I said.

""Sign her up. You never know, that might lead to somethin', for real," he said, smiling.

"Maybe."

For a moment it seemed as though we ran out of things to discuss now that we had shed tears. We began to stare at Sabrina as she played with other children on the monkey bars.

"Well, now that we've talked, I think it's time that I go speak with Sabrina," he suggested.

"She doesn't even know you. Where would you start?" I asked, frustrated.

"I can't worry about that right now. Six years has been long enough. So I think I at least owe her that," he said.

I sighed and crossed my arms. I felt so defeated. Would there always be un fightable battles in our lives that we would be destined to never overcome?

"You don't mind do you?" he asked.

"No, go ahead. Like you said, six years has been long enough."

For a moment I was skeptical. But as I saw him approach her, I became relieved. She looked at me for approval, until I gestured that he was safe. I watched them talk as he offered his hand for a handshake. She quickly accepted and smiled as she leaped onto him with a hug.

He twirled her around like a kite in the wind as she squealed in delight. Her ponytails and dress flared out like a parachute as she enjoyed her merry-go-round ride. It brought tears of joy as I watched them unite for the first time.

Before he left, Rashad handed me a business card with an Atlanta phone number on the front. His New Mexico information was written on the back.

"My flight leaves Sunday, and I start my marketin' job in Albuquerque first thing next week," he said. "That's' if I don't suffer from too much jet lag," he laughed.

"Cool, maybe Sabrina could come up and visit you. We'll have to arrange somethin'," I suggested.

"You're both welcome to come visit me. I would love to show you around."

"I don't think so," I refused.

"Cyndi, what can I say, we were just kids when we got caught up. But look at what we were blessed with," he said, referring to Sabrina. "There's a lot that I missed in her life, but now I want to make it right. I want to be there for her."

For a minute I became speechless. I wasn't sure what to say as he continued to speak. "Marry me Cyndi," he proposed. He took my hands into his.

He stared intently into my eyes making me melt all over, our eyes quickly catching up on what we'd had and what we'd lost.

"I have to think about it," I said, caught up in his trance.

"Trust me. We'll have a good life together."

"The last time you told me to trust you I ended up three months pregnant with little money in my pocket," I answered.

"Marry me, Cyndi. Marry me."

The world was spinning, I couldn't keep up. Everything was happening so fast. "I have to go," I resisted, trying to pull away.

"Cyndi!" he called, still clinging onto me.

"I have to go," I repeated.

"Cyndi, I meant what I said!" he yelled as I scooped up Sabrina and we walked away.

Chapter 23

"Who was that man, Mommy?" Sabrina asked as we rode home in the car.

I wanted to fabricate a story and tell her he was an old friend, as a protective mechanism. But I couldn't do it. I realized that it wouldn't be fair to her. Instinct was telling me not to. Instead I remained silent, as many thoughts raced inside my head.

"Mommy?" she asked, realizing that I took too long to answer.

"You may not remember this Sabrina, but a long time ago we used to live with somebody who was very evil and dangerous. But we left him and now we never have to see him again," I explained.

"I remember," Sabrina answered. "I remember when he used to always yell at you and make you cry. Why was daddy so mean?"

"Oh my God, you actually remember that?" I asked stunned.

All that time I always believed that she was safe in her make-believe world. But in reality, she was absorbing everything that happened. I suddenly began to feel guilty, wishing that I could have protected her better.

"Yeah," she answered timidly.

"So you actually remember all those times when we were always on the run looking for safety?"

"Yeah, why did he always get so mad?" she asked innocently.

"I don't know, Sabrina."

"Is he gonna come back to get us?" she asked fearfully.

"Never. He's locked away some place far away," I said, while staring at her in the rearview.

"Now, gettin' back to your question, Martina once told you when you were little that you had two daddies. One was good and the other was bad," I said.

"I know."

"Well, you just met your good daddy," I informed.

"I did?" she asked, confused.

"Yeah, he was the man in the park."

"Really?" she asked, astonished.

"Yeah."

"Cool, 'cause I like him!" she cheered.

"You do?" I asked, shocked.

It had only been 20 minutes that they'd spent together and already she'd established a bond with him. How could this be?

"Yeah, he was a lot of fun!"

"I like him too," I admitted.

Somehow at this point, I couldn't let go. Besides having Sabrina, what other type of connection did Rashad and I have?

Later that evening, Sabrina and I traveled to Brooklyn, New York. I felt this was my only way of confronting my demons. After catching the train into the city, we walked around in my old neighborhood, eating ice-cream. I took her to the foster home where I grew up. As we approached the building, my body suddenly froze.

The building was abandoned. Most of the windows and doors were boarded up with a ton of graffiti covering the exterior. The pavement that was once well-kept was now replaced with overgrown weeds and litter. I saw that one of the windows was broken and a mob of rats had infested the entire property. I almost screamed.

"What happened?" I asked out loud.

A nun walking by who overheard my reaction approached us. "That place has been shut down for more than 10 years," she said.

"You're kiddin'!" I cried. "What happened?"

"Ever since Ms. Francis..."

"I remember her," I interrupted.

"Ever since Ms. Francis passed away," the nun continued, "that place just fell apart. She suffered a stroke and became really sick, and from then on, the place just went downhill."

"But just after she passed, her son who should have taken it over was arrested for child abuse. He was reported for beating and starving some of the kids. Once he was hauled off, the kids just went wild and destroyed the place," she explained.

"Oh my God," I couldn't believe it.

"Once Big Mike was arrested, a new owner tried to fix it up, but the state unfortunately lost funding and they had to shut it down."

"What happened to the kids?" I asked.

"Some were transferred to other group home facilities, others, we don't know. There's no telling. In jail for all we know," she answered sadly. "I'm sure Ms. Francis has to be turning over in her grave by now."

"That's terrible," I said.

The nun nodded in agreement. Then she said a soft Catholic prayer, stroked Sabrina's cheek and walked away.

"Where are we, Mommy?" Sabrina asked, glancing around.

I think she felt uncomfortable now that we were out of our element. I never exposed her to this part of town since I always wanted to put it behind me. But today, I somehow had the urge to confront my past.

"Someplace where I used to live. It was very sad here, but we don't have to worry about it anymore," I said. "Now, let's go get some more ice-cream before we head back," I took her by the hand and we walked away.

At least Big Mike got what he deserved. He had it comin', I thought.

Once we returned from our four hour trip, Sabrina and I had TV dinners with mashed potatoes, baked chicken, and steamed vegetables. As soon as we finished, she took a bath make believing with her bath toys and splashing soap suds everywhere. I couldn't help but laugh as she enjoyed her recreational time making tidal waves.

After slipping into her pink pajama set, she joined me in the living room to watch her favorite cartoon. Sabrina loved watching Sponge bob Square pants. When her animated soap opera ended, I tucked her in bed.

"Good night, rug rat," I kissed her forehead.

"Good night, Mommy," she giggled while squeezing my neck.

"Did you brush your teeth?" I reminded.

Sabrina showed her pearly whites as though she were trying to prove that she was telling the truth. "Yep."

Instantly, her eyes closed and she was out. Her teddy bear was snuggled beside her, wearing a pink ribbon around its neck. I quietly rose from her bed and softly closed her door. I knew that she was worn out from our busy day. Just when I was about to step into the shower, the phone rang. I picked it up eagerly.

"What's up?" I greeted.

"Hey, baby," a familiar voice sent shivers down my spine.

"Who the hell is this?" I demanded, not wanting to hear him reveal his identity.

"Who else would call you? It's your husband."

"We never got married, Dominique!" I snapped.

Thank God we didn't!

"We could've gotten married. That was my plan you know," he said.

"What do you want Dominique?"

"I wanted to check on you and see how you were doing. I miss you."

"How did you get this number?" I asked, frantically.

All this time I thought I had a private identity.

"Come on, now. Peoplesearch.com. Did you honestly think you would get away from me that easily?" he chuckled.

"I don't know what you want Dominique, but it's over. Don't call me again. Don't send me e-mails, don't Facebook me, and don't look me up. Leave me alone! You're not even supposed to have contact with me anyway."

"I know, I know. I just wanted to hear your voice. I really miss you Cyndi. I wish I could go back and change things," he said remorsefully.

"It's too late for that! You should've thought of that when you were pistolin' me around!" I huffed.

"I was going through a lot of stuff during that time. I never told you this, but I've always struggled with bipolar disorder. But I'm now getting help for it," he said.

"Now you tell me," I said, rolling my eyes. I didn't care anymore.

"What you did to me wasn't love, Dominique. I gotta go."

"Wait!" he urged.

"What do you want?"

"Can we start over?" he begged.

"Goodbye, Dominique," I said about to drop the phone.

"You hang up that phone and there's no turning back," he warned. "You know you can't make it without me."

"You know, it's funny, 'cause I honestly used to believe that shit. But we don't need you for real. I can take care of myself!" I fired.

"Come on, let's not fight here. I know you remember some of the good times, right?" he asked.

"No, Dominique, I remember you tryin' to smack my brains out and shovin' a knife at my throat. And you know what else is fucked up?" I asked, on the verge of tears. "Sabrina remembers that shit too!"

"Wow!" he said, blown away. "OK, I didn't call to bring up bad memories. I just wanted to patch things up. Maybe one day you can forgive me."

"Go to hell Dominique! It's over! Don't call me, don't try to find me, and stay away from Sabrina!" I ordered. "I could try to have your sentence doubled if I wanted to!"

Dominique suddenly became quiet. I knew that he was still salty about serving his five year sentence for domestic violence and child endangerment with unregistered guns. There was no chance of him ever seeing freedom until 2015.

"It's over Dominique! Leave us alone!" I raged.

"I'm gonna focus on trying to make things right between us," he said sincerely.

"No, how 'bout you concentrate on not droppin' the soap, bitch!" I yelled, slamming the receiver in his ear and storming into the bathroom.

I stepped into my tub and tried to calm myself. I needed a break. Too much was going on. Rashad just tried to pop back into my life and now I get a call from Dominique. What else could happen? While marinating in my soap suds, I began to think of the next day.

It was going to be hectic for me. Sabrina was going on a field trip with her class and I had a job interview at a clinic. This meant that we had to get up earlier. I was scheduled to meet with a nursing administrator for a potential job once I completed my program. I was extremely nervous. As soon as I stepped out of the tub, the doorbell rang.

Having company at 10:30 at night was something that definitely was not planned. I had no clue who wanted to see me at this time of night. I slipped into a robe and walked to the front door. As I stared into the peephole, I had trouble recognizing my visitor.

The rainfall outside was pouring heavily, and his hat was covering part of his face. But I could tell that it was Rashad. I would never forget those luscious lips and that smooth, caramel complexion.

"Hey," I greeted as I opened the door.

"What's up?" he replied, stepping inside.

"You're all wet," I laughed.

"I know. I see that you're pretty soaked yourself," he smiled.

"I just got out of the shower," I informed.

"Oh," he never took his gaze off of me.

"Uh, I'm gonna go get you a towel," I said, trying to avoid eye contact, although I didn't want to.

His toned and beautifully tanned arms were calling to me as they glistened with raindrops. His kissable, muscular chest bulged through his soaked wife beater. I was starving for his physical attention as I stared at his sculptured abs, but I couldn't let him know it.

"I just thought I'd come to say goodbye," he said, drying off.

"Well Sabrina's gonna miss you, for sure."

"Where is she? Can I see her?" he asked eagerly.

"She's already asleep. But you can still see her. I'll tell her that you came by," I offered.

He removed his hat and soaked shirt and followed me toward her room. There was Sabrina in her precious, comfortable bed, now hugging her teddy bear. Her long, wavy hair was spread across her pillow, since her bonnet had slipped off. Sabrina's room was decorated in her favorite colors pink and white.

Her comforter, valances and walls were pink, and her soft carpet and wicker furniture were white. He saw that she had a tea set with her dolls at her table. Every doll was dressed in a fancy dress with a ribbon.

"She's beautiful isn't she?" he whispered as we stared through the narrow crack of her door.

"She has your eyes," I said.

"You really think she's gonna miss me?" he asked.

"I know she will. She feels a connection with you already," I assured.

"Does her mother feel a connection with me too?" he asked, now closing the door.

"Rashad, we talked about this already," I said.

"I know what you said. But how do you *really* feel?"

It was as though he could read my thoughts. Maybe my eyes revealed my true feelings, even as my words expressed the opposite. But I couldn't lie to him.

"I'm scared," I admitted, tears now forming.

"You don't have to be scared. I want to protect you. Let me love you, Cyndi. Just give me that chance," he pulled me toward him.

Chapter 24

I leaned into his embrace and let him kiss the side of my neck. Our bodies were starved for physical attention. Before he continued to caress me, he stared into my eyes again and then removed my robe. Our communication continued through eye contact as my garment hit the floor. Immediately I went to unfasten his shorts and remove his boxers. He stepped out of his clothes that fell to his ankles, as I let his tongue travel down my breasts. Before I knew it, he picked me up and carried me into my bedroom. I wrapped my legs around him as Rashad kicked the door shut and carried me to the bed. He gently laid me down and turned me onto my stomach.

He kissed me up and down the curve of my back, trying to kiss away my ugly scars from Dominique's abuse. Years ago, I was nervous when I first made love to Rashad. He was my first. But today, I was ready to put those fears aside. I didn't want to stop him. Rashad turned me onto my back and kissed my finger tips. Soon he began to kiss my inner thighs and went to devour my womanhood, scrumptiously. He grabbed my thighs and held me tightly as I squirmed.

Once I reached my climax, I heard him whisper that he would return momentarily, and he slipped out of the room. When he returned, Rashad came back with my scented candles and rose petals from my potpourri dish. He also had my massage oil from the bathroom, and strawberries and a can of whipped cream from the kitchen. I let him light the candles and scatter the rose petals while I laid in bed in sexual anticipation. I could tell that he wanted our environment to be perfect, but I was ready for him to hurry back. Shortly, he joined me on the bed and continued his flow.

There we were, making love late at night, as the rain poured and thundered in the summer, night sky. The candles flickered, the rose petals released their sweet scent, and the massage oil, caressed our skin. The group 112's older hits Peaches and Cream and You Already Know were on repeat as the sheets clung to our sweaty bodies.

We rubbed each other and moaned with pleasure, enjoying every minute that we spent with each other. Tears of pleasure rolled down my cheeks, as Rashad had me straddle him and pulled me toward him. I felt him push deep. He grabbed my shoulders tightly and I didn't let go. Our passion lasted for three hours, but it felt like eternity. As our ecstasy ended, he completed my ecstasy with a full baby oil massage. I felt him kiss my back as he massaged my rear, with Silk's tune, Lose Control, playing in the background.

"I love you Cyndi," he whispered in my ear.

His words and affection were perfect music to my ears. But I knew shortly afterward, his actions would be the opposite. I couldn't go through this again. Not another emotional rollercoaster, when I'd been doing so well. I finally decided to put a stop to it before he would.

"You should leave," I replied.

"What?"

"Please don't make this any harder for me. Just go," I ordered, rolling onto my side. I couldn't look him in the face.

"But Cyndi, I only came here to..."

"I know what you came here for," I interrupted. "But it's not gonna happen. The fun times are over. Now I'll ask you again, leave."

"Damn, I don't know what to say," he said painfully.

"Look, you popped back into my life like a prince in a fairy tale, but it's not gonna work. So, I want you to pop out the same way you popped in," I said. "Goodbye Rashad," I said pulling the covers over my head.

He stood in the doorway for a moment, then he finally walked out. I heard him dress himself in the hallway and call someone from his cell. When he finished he returned to my room.

"I just called for a cab. I didn't come here to hurt you, Cyndi. I was hopin' that we could make amends," he said, his voice fading.

I could tell that he was hurting as much as I was. But it was too late to go back. Too much turmoil from our past had spoiled our potential future.

"I know you did," I said.

"Will you tell Sabrina that I said goodbye and that I love her?" he asked.

"Lock the door before you leave," I commanded, my back still facing him.

"Damn. So, I guess it's like that, huh?" he asked as he walked out.

I heard the sound of a car horn and then his phone rang. As he answered it, he was already out the door. The minute he left, I jumped up and ran to look out the window. Just when I was about to return to bed, I noticed a folded piece of paper on the floor by the door. I picked it up and realized that he left his ID and itinerary. They must have fallen out of his pocket.

"Rashad!" I called, running outside.

But it was too late. He was gone. I saw his cab cruise down the long, dark road and turn the corner. Damn!

"Rashad! Rashad!" I yelled, hoping he could hear me. I tried to run after him as if the car would stop. But it didn't.

Not only did I just ruin our intimacy but I chased away the man who I would forever love. Plus I had his ID and itinerary. I flopped onto the wet grass and cried. I really fucked up this time. We didn't use any contraceptives again and now he was gone. But, tomorrow morning I would rush to my nearest pharmacy and purchase a box of Plan B. I loved Rashad, but I couldn't tell him. It was time to move on.

My T-shirt became soaked and dirty with grass stains, but I didn't care. I sat on my front lawn and cried as the rain continued its heavy downpour. Thunder and lightning flickered around me, but I didn't budge. Just when I was about to run inside to call him, I heard a voice.

The storm was loud but I heard his voice so clear. I looked up and saw Rashad running toward me. I sprung up and ran to him with my arms eager to wrap around him one more time. The sprint seemed forever, but we continued running until we joined again.

"You left your ID and itinerary," I said.

"I know. I didn't realize it until we hit the highway. But then I realized that I couldn't do it. I couldn't leave," he said.

"You mean you're not leavin'?" I asked.

"Not without you."

I was speechless.

"That's if you will. You will come with me, won't you?" he pleaded.

"Yes," I answered determinedly.

"I want you to be my wife, Cyndi. Will you marry me?"

"Yes."

"You will?" he asked, excitedly.

"Yes!" I stared intently into his eyes.

"Well, let's do it then!" he cried. He picked me up and swung me around like a helicopter.

Three months later...

Rashad and I were married within three months. Although it was somewhat short notice, we still had an elaborate wedding. I wanted us to fly to Las Vegas and do it the quick way, but Rashad wanted to have a traditional wedding.

"I really wanna do it right," he said. "I owe you that."

Eventually I agreed. After all, he did put me through a lot. We had our ceremony at a church in Providence, Rhode Island. Sabrina was my flower girl and Martina and two of my high school friends, Sonia and Su, were my bridesmaids. Rashad's cousin, Derrick, and Martina's husband Devon, were the groomsmen. My mother was my matron of honor. She had her new boyfriend, Wesley walk me down the aisle. My other friend Antoinette sung a solo. I wore an ivory wedding gown in a contemporary style.

It had ruffles along the skirt and fastened like a corset around my bosom. The gown was strapless and had crystals along the front and back, with a train and matching veil. My hair was twisted up into a French twist and I wore light make-up. All the bridesmaids wore similarly styled gowns in silver and carried matching bouquets. My mother's and Sabrina's gowns were in a champagne color and they carried white flowers. Rashad wore a white tuxedo and his groomsmen wore grey. As we exchanged vows, I became teary-eyed. A flood of emotions occurred all at once.

After the ceremony, we had our reception at The Hyatt, with lots of food and festivities. When it was time to throw the bouquet, Su ended up catching it, which made Antoinette angry.

"Oh, no she didn't!" she huffed sarcastically.

"Sorry, your loss," Su laughed.

"Um, we'll just see about that!" Antoinette said, rolling her eyes.

Everyone had a laugh and then participated in a line dance, as Cupid's and V.I.C.'s songs, Cupid Shuffle and Wobble, played. As we danced, the photographer snapped dozens of photos. He took so many, I was sure that we would have enough to fill two photo albums.

Toward the end of the reception, Rashad and I flew off for a three-week honeymoon in Jamaica and Barbados. Sabrina stayed with both her grandmothers during that time. I wanted to give them a chance to bond. I was truly happy to be married to Rashad.

Sabrina adjusted well and was excited to have her real father around. Once we returned from our honeymoon,

Sabrina and I moved to Albuquerque, New Mexico with Rashad. He pursued his marketing and film directing careers and I continued to pursue my medical profession. Eventually, I was hired as a health educator at a teen clinic.

My job was to provide outreach services and coordinate prevention programs at different organizations. I was ecstatic to be offered the position. I knew this would help lead me to my ultimate goal of one day having a healthcare agency of my own. Sabrina continued to strive for great grades in school and made a lot of friends. At times she would come home and share exciting stories of the social activities that she engaged in.

"I think I got a new best friend now, mommy!" she cried.

"Good for you. What's her name?"

"Willow," she answered. "Just like Will Smith's daughter."

"Can she sing like her?" I chuckled.

"I dunno," Sabrina giggled.

I watched her run off with her new friends to join them for a bike ride. It didn't take much to excite or dazzle Sabrina. She was so innocent. Hopefully she and Willow would remain friends at heart forever, just as Martina and I had.

Martina and Devon had been through some rough times themselves. Martina had cheated so many times and it one day caught up with her. Devon contracted an STD from her that she had got from Tre, the guy she met at the mall years before. She and Devon were devastated, and she was caught red-handed. They spent several months apart, but attended couples therapy together. Martina truly loved Devon, but had a hard time admitting that she battled a sex addiction.

After Devon gave her an ultimatum, Martina got herself together through rehab and counseling. Although, Devon had doubts and trust issues gnawing in the back of his mind, he still loved her. Eventually they chose to fight for their marriage and started over, even having a new marriage commitment ceremony. Not long after, they conceived two sons, Dionne and Diego. The boys were 10 months apart and favored Devon. Devon decided to pursue electronic and electrical engineering, and Martina became an elementary teacher in English as a second language. My mother and I still remained close. She would occasionally visit us or have Sabrina fly to New Jersey for trips. Occasionally I thought of my half-sister, Brittney.

My mother had made several attempts to contact her, but Brittney never responded. I knew this hurt my mother, but she would sometimes respond with a shrug, "I ain't worried about it for real. It's just gonna take some time that's all," she would say. "Look how far we've come."

Brittney eventually became an architect and married a senior citizen. He was a retired judge from Texas. Surely, she married this man for money, because they had absolutely nothing in common. He was three times her age. I once came across her Facebook page that bragged about an event she was sponsoring. It read:

All members of the Chadwick Organization are invited to a banquet sponsored by Mrs. Brittney Leshawn Kramer-Stevens. Contestants participating in the charity raffle will receive guest passes for weekend excursions at the Cedar Lodge in Providence, Rhode Island. A 70th birthday bash also will be included, in honor of former Judge Charlie Stevens.

Visitors are expected to attend the event in black and white formal attire.

I wanted to slap the flighty arrogance out of her. How typical of her, I thought. She never had children and never worked a hard day in her life. Would she ever become independent? So much for being a part of my sister's life. She had a beautiful niece that she could easily establish a bond with, but probably never would. But that part of my life didn't matter. I had a real family that was willing to love and accept me eagerly.

I had my mother, who was supportive. I had my husband Rashad, who shared my tumultuous past; yet he was willing to start a better future with me. I also had my beautiful daughter, Sabrina who was a blessing sent from God. And, I had my best friend Martina, who would always be the sister that I never truly had with Brittney.

I once said to Rashad, "If we ever have a son, I want to call him Taj."

"Sure," he agreed.

I knew Rashad was inquisitive of my request, but he never asked any questions. And I never gave an explanation. As the years passed, I was fortunate to watch my daughter grow into a beautiful woman. At age 12, she joined the track team and participated in gymnastics and figure skating.

Sabrina had always been athletic and active, so I encouraged her to pursue all that she could. There was never a day that Rashad or I were not proud of her. We never had a second child. But for once in our lives, I finally could say that we were truly happy and blessed. Life had turned out to be good, despite the ups and downs along the way.

Remarks:

I wrote this novel, because I enjoy writing stories about scenarios that teens can relate to. Some teens may encounter situations that are too uncomfortable to discuss with adults, such as, peer pressure and promiscuity. Parents are uncomfortable addressing these problems, when communication with teens becomes a barrier between them. My books are an outlet for teens, if personally expressing their emotions becomes too complicated. I feel parents can also refer to my books as a resource. My real-world plots may give them a better perspective on how to communicate with their daughters.

In addition, some girls may encounter additional problems such as, under reported or unreported cases of domestic violence, and/or teen pregnancy. In these cases, girls may not have an advocate in which to confide. Therefore, they may feel their only option is to "deal with their problems themselves." Often when this occurs, girls may suppress their depression, thus elevating unresolved issues. As they become adults, this vicious cycle of victimization may continue. Yet, as young women read my story, they may recognize that they're not alone with these problems. The realization that another victim has experienced these exact traumas, or possibly worse; may help remediate feelings of "aloneness." However, after reading the story, *Cyndi,* perhaps young women and parents may identify better strategies to advocate for themselves and other victims.

Cyndi

Jamila D. Smith

Made in the USA
Middletown, DE
24 December 2022

17564907R00136